Clement Scott, Arthur J Smythe

The Life of William Terriss

Clement Scott, Arthur J Smythe

The Life of William Terriss

ISBN/EAN: 9783337333027

Printed in Europe, USA, Canada, Australia, Japan

Cover: Foto ©Raphael Reischuk / pixelio.de

More available books at **www.hansebooks.com**

THE LIFE OF
WILLIAM TERRISS

Actor

BY ARTHUR J. SMYTHE
WITH AN INTRODUCTION
BY CLEMENT SCOTT

WESTMINSTER
ARCHIBALD CONSTABLE & CO
2 WHITEHALL GARDENS
1898

Table of Contents

v

List of Illustrations

vii

AN APPRECIATION

By Clement Scott

A FTER a roving, adventurous life, here, there, and everywhere, now on board some trading vessel bound for the far east, now exploring the Falkland Islands of all places in the world, William Terriss, the best and most loyal friend man ever had, found himself eventually on the boards of a London theatre, determined, if possible, to distinguish himself as an actor. His early career, which combined the frank recklessness of the sailor with its breezy good nature, which he retained to the last, with the daring of the impulsive discoverer, will be recorded elsewhere. He was fond of relating one pathetic tale, which proves how sudden and quick were his impulses. He was the owner of a small cottage in a pleasant London suburb, and suddenly resolved to be off and away on one of his harum-scarum expeditions. His mind once made up, the pro-

ject was instantly carried into execution. Breakfast over one morning, he promptly packed up
his traps, sick to death of the confinement of
London life and its want of freedom. He left
the place just as it was, closed the shutters,
locked the door, and gave the key of the tenant-
less house to a neighbour. In due time the
wanderer returned again, opened the cottage door,
found the breakfast things just as he had left
them, but on the now soiled tablecloth—a skeleton! A skeleton of what? Well, the skeleton
of a poor hungry cat, that he had accidentally
locked into the empty house when he went away.
The wretched creature had lapped up the last
drop of milk and then lay down to die of starva-
tion. It was said that my old friend was an
unemotional man, but he never told this story
without the tears coming to his eyes; for, like
all good and brave fellows, he was passionately
fond of animals.

But to return to the theatre. It was in 1868
that I first saw young Terriss on the stage, in
the very small part of " Lord Cloudwrays " in

AN APPRECIATION

Robertson's *Society*; but the character was insignificant, and it was no test of his power. But at the opening of Drury Lane Theatre, on September 21st, 1872, I saw and appreciated on the other side of the footlights a young actor who was destined to become one of the most deservedly popular artists of my time. The play was Sir Walter Scott's *Lady of the Lake*, dramatized by Andrew Halliday. E. L. Blanchard briefly records of this production: "Beverley scenery very good; the rest very bad." In the cast were Harry Sinclair ("Roderick Dhu"), James Fernandez ("Fitzjames"), Maria B. Jones ("Helen"), Mrs. Aynsley Cooke ("Lady Margaret"), J. Dewhurst ("Douglas"), Rosenthal ("Brian the Seer"), and "Malcolm"—William Terriss.

I was at that time writing for *The Observer* as well as in the *Daily Telegraph*. I find the following words recorded in the former paper in connection with the first important performance of Terriss, and they are interesting as showing that even then, six and twenty years ago, one of my favourite hobbies was stage elocution. Having

xi

described the play and the mounting of it, I said :—

" It would be ungracious to pick the acting to pieces, because all the artists had such scant opportunity of exhibiting their talent. They were, from first to last, subordinate to and hard pressed by the scene-painter, the carpenter, and the costumier. But fresh and pleasant, active and intelligent, enthusiastic and natural, stood out among all the rest the ' Malcolm Graeme ' of Mr. W. Terriss, a young actor, who has now made a very fair start, and will, no doubt, do uncommonly well. The contrast between the natural and manly declamation of this young actor and the old-fashioned stilted style of some of his fellows was very striking, and it is really pleasant to find any one determined to speak as ordinary people speak, on the boards of a theatre, wherein strange tones and emphasis prevail."

Poor Terriss has often told me that it was this criticism and this first praise that settled his vocation in life. He never forgot it. He never ceased to be grateful for it, and when in

AN APPRECIATION

course of time we met outside the walls of a theatre in those delightful Bohemian days, we formed a firm friendship that was never broken for a single hour. It has recently been said, with some emphasis, that this example is by no means exceptional, that actors and actresses never forget kindnesses done to them, always treasure the memory of the helping hand, and forget the awkward and occasional blame when contrasted with the almost continuous praise. I regret to say that has not been my experience after a career of forty years. I say emphatically that the attitude of a frank, outspoken, fearless man like Terriss was extremely exceptional—in fact, quite unique in my experience. The critic, however enthusiastic when he can conscientiously praise, must at odd and rare times be the natural enemy of the able, conscientious, and disappointed actor. But in no other career, untarnished by egotism and vanity, is there so much treachery. To our face we are angels; behind our back, devils. We are offered the loving cup, and as we drink—the dagger; and it is the assassin who dies.

AN APPRECIATION

During his theatrical adventures, I did not always agree with the methods of my friend, particularly in a character that either did not suit him or which I had seen better performed by others. One cannot obliterate memories. I had seen both Alfred Wigan and Walter Lacy as "Chateau Renaud," in the *Corsican Brothers*, and I thought and said that they were both more convincing to me than Terriss. No doubt he did not like it at the time. But he did not go into a corner and sulk, and tear his hair and swear or curse me by all his gods as others have been apt to do. A difference of opinion in court made no "kink" in our friendship. The case over, however much as we differed, we could go along the Strand arm-in-arm, as opposing barristers and others continually do. The "Chateau Renaud" at the Lyceum was no doubt a bitter draught to swallow, but this genuine, manly fellow never forgot my appreciation of "Malcolm Graeme." I heard afterwards of his disappointment, his bitter grief, when the "Chateau Renaud" was critically treated. He had said, "This will be the success of my life!" But it was not. He treated the comparative difficulty with philosophy. He did not go into the nearest club, curse his critic, and make a fool of himself. I never met a man in any class of life who in every action showed such thorough contempt for toadying or backbiting, and the terrible artistic habit of saying one thing to your face and another behind your back was unknown to him. He stood no nonsense from anybody, and that was why he was respected and loved by the majority of men and women. He recognised that courtesy and discipline are requisite in every theatre. He would show the one and regard the other. But he would stand no non-sense from the highest actor or the greatest person in the land. Had Terriss been old enough to act with Macready, and there hap-pened to be any difference of opinion between them, I don't think the younger actor would have come off second best. In society, at country houses, even at a very ceremonial court,

AN APPRECIATION

this popular and daring fellow soon established his independence and power. His attitude was received with a stare of astonishment at first, but as there was no impudence in it, but mere dare-devilry, the Terriss manner soon won for him the very warmest friendships in every class of society.

The one day of the year that was especially dear to this young-hearted and engaging creature was in the glow of summer time when the Drury Lane Fund gave its annual outing. I have often been privileged to be the guest of William Terriss on these occasions, and no matter where we went or found ourselves, in the buttercup fields round Stoke Poges Church, on the river on a launch going upwards from Maidenhead to Henley, or at dinner afterwards at Skindles, or at the Grey-hound at Richmond, Terriss was always the life and soul of the party, and we had some bright and merry times when Charles Warner, James Fernandez, and our old friend were prime officers of this distinguished gathering. It was at one of these yearly festivals that old Benjamin Webster took the chair at the Sunday Richmond dinner. His age was great, his memory failing a little, and his once powerful mind occasionally wandering. I remember well how, to the astonishment of us all, the grand old man stood up, raising his wine glass with a feeble, faltering hand, and said : " The King ! God Bless Him ! " He imagined he was living in another age and in another reign.

The next year, as we were driving Kennington way one lovely Sunday morning in the summer time, Terriss, in his genial fashion, proposed that we should all stop and pay our respects to the venerable Master of the Fund, who was fading slowly away. Benjamin Webster lived and had done so for years in an old-fashioned house in a secluded garden at the back of Kennington Church. There we found him sitting with a little child on his knee—his last born. By a curious coincidence the veteran comedian was sitting under a picture of himself when a child on his mother's knee. The two children might have been painted from the same model. Whilst they were all shaking hands with and congratulating the " Master,"

AN APPRECIATION

Terriss nudged me and proposed an exploration into the old garden. A curious sight presented itself. The grass and herbage came up to our knees, the trees were tangled and twisted together, reminding us of the wood where "Sleeping Beauty" rested when discovered by her lover, and in an out-house we found an old-fashioned carriage that had probably not been used for years. The mud was still on the wheels caused by some forgotten journey from the old Haymarket or Webster's Adelphi.

William Terriss was a popular actor in every sense of the word. He was beloved by young and old alike. In his thoroughly English method there was perhaps not much subtlety or insight into the lights and shades of character; in his honest sentiment, displayed so often in melodrama, the pathos and heart throbs may occasionally have been considered superficial, but he brought on to the stage a buoyant individuality, a joyous manner, the essential spirit of good nature, a handsome face, a light active figure, and a resonant voice that could be heard in every corner of the largest theatre. Such a voice is a temptation to any actor, for he loves to hear it echo around the theatre and to feel its influence. I somehow think that the finest thing he did in his career was his "Squire Thornhill," in the *Olivia* of W. G. Wills. He might have walked out of the text of the *Vicar of Wakefield*, handsome, reckless, cruel, cynical, assertive, the very man that an Olivia would have loved, for it is one of the privileges or eccentricities of good women to fall in love with dare-devil, handsome, unscrupulous men. Some women, like the Irishman's car horse, "love to be oppressed." His "William" in *Black-Eyed Susan* was a wonderful performance for a man of his age. He danced the hornpipe like a lad of eighteen. But his soul hankered after serious parts in solemn plays. I was partly responsible for providing him with such a character in *The Swordsman's Daughter*. In it there were fine moments for Terriss. But the public refused to accept their favourite as an old man, and shuddered at the thought that this bright fellow should be paralysed even in a play.

AN APPRECIATION

They wanted him as he was, ever young, and did not care to see a line on his handsome, expressive face or a grey hair in his shapely head. He was indeed a bitter loss to the English stage, and at present he has no successor.

Of the cruel and dastard blow that with such awful suddenness deprived my dear and faithful friend of life, I forbear to speak. I had seen him but a short time before in his dressing-room at the Adelphi, where we had many a confidential chat between the acts, or when his favourite dresser was rubbing him down after the hard work was over. He looked like some splendid young athlete, with not one superfluous ounce of flesh about him, and with a fair, smooth skin like satin. A more symmetrical man for his age I have never seen. And he was doomed to depart before his oldest friend. I was in Paris in great trouble when I heard the news. The shock I felt then, I have not recovered to this hour. And I lost my friend at the very moment when I could have counted on his brave and loyal championship to counteract much that was mean,

AN APPRECIATION

ungrateful—yes, and unmanly too. All that was opposed to the temperament of William Terriss the actor—*and gentleman!* Terriss was not the honest fellow in an instant to turn friendship into loathing and contempt. He certainly would have been the last man in the world to countenance the strange acts of some of his vainglorious companions. But, although we were to have gone down into the country together a few days after what proved to be the fatal one for him, we were destined never to meet again. Lightly rest the turf above him!

A few of the letters written to me in the days of our early friendship, and some of the very last he ever penned to me, may be of interest to all who admired his outspoken candour, his honest friendship, and his splendid manly nature. Some of these will show how, in a mysterious manner, the knowledge of death — sudden or otherwise—was ever present to him. No end of a year, no anniversary ever came to me without some affectionate greeting from this staunch and loyal friend. God rest his soul!

AN APPRECIATION

DEAR SCOTT,—

You ask me, have I *decided finally*? I regret to say it does not rest in *my power* to decide at all. Otherwise you know the best of my inclinations only too well. I went to see Clarke again on receipt of your letter, and the only answer I can get from him is that "he can give me no decided answer either aye or nay, as he will most likely want me, etc."

I'm afraid that you must look upon my coming as a hope forlorn. You know how I must regret it?

I think I shall finally decide to go to " Wallacks " in the autumn, unless you will take the trouble to get me to the " Prince of Wales."

My part in the Crisis, as you say, is so vague and undefined that I can do nothing for it or with it.

Wishing you and yours a merry Xmas and many of them,

Believe me, yours always,

W. TERRISS.

Please send me a carte-de-visite of yourself, if you will spare one. I should much esteem the favour.

ADELPHI THEATRE.

[*A few months before his death.*]

MY DEAR CLEM,—

Will you kindly write on this picture something more than your autograph, so that my children may, when I

AN APPRECIATION

and you are gone, know the many years the poor actor
and great critic were ever friends, 1870 to 1897.

To me last night your not coming was a bitter disappointment. I personally care not a "curse" for the
opinions of any one but yourself, good or bad, and
your absence was a great loss to the whole thing as
far as acting was concerned.

I do not alter my opinion one iota about the play as
a work of dramatic interest—it's the "poorest . . ." all
round I have ever heard, and it . . . The piece is
beautifully dressed and mounted, but the stuffing is bad
and . . . You'll judge for yourself some day, and bear
the same opinion as I do.

I am sorry seeing about your good wife's father. I
hope it's nothing serious. Commend me to her and all
good wishes,

Always sincerely yours,

WILL.

I'll send for the picture to-morrow night.

LYCEUM THEATRE,

April 15, 1894.

It is useless, dear Scott, my ever writing to thank you
for your kindly thoughts, which you always express towards me in my work in the *Telegraph*, but it pleases me
to do so. Again, thanks ; I appreciate it.

We are travelling along the road of life together, and
it is a ray of sunshine to know one has always a well-

xxiii

AN APPRECIATION

wisher and a friend. Life is *not* like a game of pool, for we can't *star one*, yet in my transient theatrical career I am ever glad that I merit your good opinion.

All good wishes.

Sincerely yours,

WILL TERRISS.

LYCEUM THEATRE,

June 14, 1893.

MY DEAR OLD FRIEND,—

I send you a few lines to *welcome you home* again, and with the sincere wish that your future and your wife's will be one unalloyed pleasure and happiness.

I send herewith a "Theatre Magazine," where in an interview with me you will see I refer to the fact that you were the cause of my being an actor. It may interest you. God bless you!

WILL TERRISS.

LYCEUM THEATRE,

December 31, 1890.

Life is a railroad with many stations and a terminus. We have travelled a long way together, and may it be our good fortune to travel together a long way yet. But I pause for a moment on the threshold of a New Year to send you Greeting and sincere wishes for a happy and prosperous time in 1891.

WILL TERRISS.

AN APPRECIATION

ADELPHI THEATRE.
Why, certainly, dear Clem. Thursday supper, I shall be with you. With you and Johnnie it is indeed Old Times, Old Friends, and I trust till the curtain rings down.

WILL.

October 21, 1896.

27, GREAT QUEEN STREET, W.C.,
October 14, 1882.

MY DEAR SCOTT,—

To me it is always a double pleasure to acknowledge your very kind notices of my performances. For this reason—that I have received your praise and likewise your condemnation. I have always felt that your criticisms are just ; and whether you praise or condemn me I bow to your decision, because I respect your ability, and have always firmly believed in practical as well as theoretical knowledge, which you so undoubtedly possess with regard to all things appertaining to our profession.

I have noticed, however, that I have always received at your hands the minimum of condemnation and the maximum of praise ; and it is really to me, when I have been fortunate enough to please you, a sincere pleasure to read your very kind remarks on my poor ability, but it is a far greater pleasure to find myself year after year penning you my heartiest and warmest thanks for your kind and generous praise.

It would be absurd for me to simply thank you in

AN APPRECIATION

words only, without they came from the heart; and I can assure you in this, as in every other instance when I have written to you, they have done so.

Thus respect for your criticisms gradually has given way to regard to the being, and I sincerely hope that I may long be numbered amongst those who can grasp you by the hand, and may lay claim to that word "friend" in all its true meaning.

Believe me, dear Scott,

Yours most sincerely,

WILLIAM TERRISS.

ADELPHI THEATRE.

MY DEAR OLD SCOTT,—

If I owe much of my success to my own earnest endeavours, I owe still more to the ever-generous and loving support you have ever tendered me. Words do not convey the gratitude I feel for the favours you have ever conferred on me since my earliest efforts, fifteen years ago.

I am deeply sensitive of your generous sympathy and encouragement, and have much to thank you for. Perhaps the day may yet come when I may repay you. I hope it will.

A Happy Christmas to you and yours, and every blessing.

WILL TERRISS.

AN APPRECIATION

ADELPHI THEATRE,

December 31, 1894.

Only a grasp of the hand, old friend, and happy to know, as year passes year, that your kindly feeling is un-diminished. May you and (I now add) your charming wife enjoy, in the year which dawns this morn, every happiness, and health and prosperity. Such is the wish of your friend,

WILL TERRISS.

ST. MILDREDS HOTEL,

WESTGATE-ON-SEA,

KENT.

July 23, 1894.

MY DEAR OLD FRIEND,—

I thought it would be interesting news for you that my girl Ellaline will sustain the part of "Elaine" when *King Arthur* is produced at the Lyceum Theatre at Xmas, Mr. Irving having specially engaged her—so a member of the name of Terriss will still be associated at the historic Lyceum.

I hope ere many weeks elapse to see your face across the footlights at the Old Adelphi. With regards and compliments to Mrs. Scott,

Believe me, sincerely yours,

WILL TERRISS.

I am staying down here for three weeks. Need I say how delightful it is once more to breathe the ozone—for

AN APPRECIATION

why should life all labour be? Time onward driveth fast,
and in a little time our lips are dumb.
Let us alone!

But, alas! that is just what Fate would not allow.
Let us alone! They never will, for our trusted
friends become our enemies and the best of men
falls to a dastard, and so-called murderous knife.
The hand that we have clasped in friendship, and
into which money has been poured in abundance,
takes up the butcher's knife and slays! It was
the experience of William Terriss, and it is
that of all who have studied the bitter life into
which such generous creatures are flung—and
killed!

CHAPTER I

EARLY DAYS

THERE is an old saw whose specious ring of truth has furnished it with a certain amount of vitality, which states that " the boy is father to the man "; yet if any proof were needed to show how untrustworthy these same old saws sometimes are, no better could be found than that provided by the early life of the subject of this memoir, an early life that gave little or no promise of its possessor ever attaining the honourable and well-deserved position he subsequently held among the histrionic artists of the closing years of the century. And yet the spirit of wandering, the love of change and excitement, and the constant seeking after something new, were but the means working to the end ; since few there are who will not admit that travel, experience, a deep insight into human nature both good and ill, gained in many quarters of the globe, accompanied by a due share of adventures, are a splendid stock in trade for one called upon to portray in his own person the attributes, the characteristics, the manners, and the idiosyncrasies of a hundred diverse personages, either culled from the pages of history or mere creations of the writer's brain.

William Charles James Lewin was born at 7, Circus Road, St. John's Wood, on 20th February, 1847. His father, George Herbert Lewin, though called to the Bar and having chambers in Pall Mall, practised but little, and died when his third son, William, was ten years old. His grandfather, Thomas Lewin, was private secretary to Warren Hastings in Calcutta, and he was by family ties connected with George Grote, the eminent historian of Greece. Thus it would appear that there was no lack of brains in the family; and though this particular feature was not exemplified in the early years of the future actor, yet in his case they were undoubtedly present, it may be lying dormant and maturing, until he discovered his real vocation in

AN EARLY PHOTOGRAPH

life, when they asserted themselves, and enabled him to win the position he subsequently enjoyed.

The life of William Terriss (or as we shall continue to call him, for the present, William Lewin) commences, for the public, with his entry on the stage ; but it may not be without interest to glance briefly at the years preceding this, and learn something of his doings, wanderings, and adventures which so eminently aided him in the career he subsequently adopted.

His early years were passed at St. John's Wood, Lewisham, and Clapham, and at seven years of age he was a Blue Coat boy, migrating two years later to a school at Littlehampton. It was from this establishment that he wrote to his elder brother, Dr. Friend Lewin, one of the very few early letters of his that remain.

"LITTLEHAMPTON,

"*Sept.* 29*th*, 1857.

"DEAR FRIEND,—

"I hope you are quite well. I received your letter quite safe. Will you send me a Picture of your Collage, because I want to show it to the boys.

Hopeing that you will receive my letter. I am verry happy. I have lots of stamps, so i can wright to you. I have sent you a shilling. I hope you will have it quite safe with my best love. And belive me your affectionate Brother

" WILLE."

The writing is decidedly good for a boy of ten, and beyond a slip or two in the spelling there is nothing to find fault with, while the gift of the shilling—a large sum to a lad of his age—shows an affectionate kindly feeling towards his brother, and marks a trait in his character which was ever present throughout his life—quiet generosity.

From Littlehampton, he went to Windermere College, then presided over by a Mr. Puckle, a relation of the Lewins. Here his brother Friend, known to his intimates as Bob, and two cousins were among his schoolfellows, and here it was that he engaged in his first regular fight, which might be described as quite a family affair, since the antagonists were the cousins William and Mortimer, with their respective brothers Friend and Lionel as seconds. The scene of the encounter was a space behind some bushes at

THE SCHOOL, LITTLEHAMPTON, 1858

the far end of the playground, and the fight was carried out with all due formalities. Round after round was contested, and it was only when it became apparent that neither could gain any material advantage that the seconds interfered, and brought the contest to a close ; and, as is usually the case in school fights, the combatants were the best of friends ever afterwards.

A second letter of young Lewin's exists, and, as will be seen, it was written when at this school. It bears no date, but being addressed to the same brother as the previous one after he had left the establishment, it must have been a year or two later than the first one. The handwriting is more formed, and the spelling is correct. It is a true schoolboy's letter.

" WINDERMERE COLLEGE,
" WESTMORLAND.

" MR DEAR FRIEND,—

" We have begun cricket, and I am in the fifth eleven. I have a good lot of marbles, and and I have got a nice little flask. I don't think I told you that I had a fight with Farie, a new fellow, about

as big as Rushton, and Jip Gibson was my
second; and I think I fought very well, consider-
ing you were not there. Jump (his cousin Lionel)
and Morty backed me, and I nearly got my head
broken. I wish you had been there. I am getting
on pretty well, and how are you? Is your tutor
a good one?

"Love to all.

"And believe me,

"My dear brother,

"Your affectionate Brother,

"WILLIE.

"Write soon."

From Windermere Lewin went to Bruce Castle
School, Tottenham, an establishment which has
turned out a number of well-known public men;
and his education finished by his running away,
on getting into some boyish scrape, in which the
arm of one of his fellow-scholars was broken, and
appearing in the evening at the house of his life-
long friend, Mr. Graves, in Bayswater.

School days having ended, it now became a

question what profession he should adopt ; and the
mercantile marine having been decided on, a berth
as midshipman was obtained for him on one of
Messrs. Green & Co.'s ships. An idea has got
about that he was at one time in the Royal Navy,
but this was not so. It probably arose from the
fact that for a fortnight before he sailed he used
to parade Bayswater in the glory of his new
middy's uniform. His relations went down to
Gravesend to see him off, and the next news his
mother received of him, as she was congratulating
herself that her somewhat erratic and wayward boy
was safely under strict discipline for a time, was a
telegram from Plymouth, saying he had left his
ship, as seafaring life did not suit him. The real
facts of the case were that, after beating down
Channel for a fortnight, he had become tired of
the monotony, and when the ship anchored for the
night in Plymouth harbour, he had managed to
come to terms with a boatman, who, under cover
of the darkness, put him ashore.

With this escapade ended his very short connection with the sea, and what may be called his

boyhood—a boyhood which has been described by
one, who probably knew him better than any one
else at this period of his life, as restless. He was
no reader, as some boys are ; the bent of his mind
was action. He *must* be doing something ; he
could not rest quiet for long ; and if there was no
handy legitimate safety-valve for his spirits, then
mischief was equally acceptable. And to the end
of his life this trait was ever apparent. His literature consisted of the daily and theatrical papers,
and beyond books which were recommended to him
as possible aids to the conception and representation of the characters that fell to his lot, there
were very few indeed that he read. He would
sit smoking and chatting to you for a time, but
very soon he would propose a game of chess or
cards, or it may be a stroll. His mind *must* be
at work on something, it mattered not what.
Even in his early days he did not seem to know
the meaning of fear ; it had no place in his nature.
As a proof of this, in order to bring his mother
to what *he* considered reason, he, one day, lay full
length, swaying backwards and forwards, almost on

AT SEA

the edge of a very steep slated roof, a fall from which meant certain death.

It was now clear to those most interested in his welfare that little was to be looked for in the way of a seafaring life. The ocean could not offer sufficient inducement to charm this wayward spirit, and a hope revived that he might settle down to a quiet home life. His ideas, however, ran in the opposite direction, and notwithstanding the wise counsel of those dear to him, he cast in his lot with the gay, frivolous world, deeming it somewhat prosy and absurd to commence a hum-drum existence at so early a stage of his life. Just about this time, when he was seventeen, he came in for a moderate legacy from an uncle, and as if under the impression that it would last for ever, he spent money freely, and enjoyed the life of a rich young man about town. Among other luxuries he set up a trap of his own design, which has since been described by one who knew it as "a kind of glorified milk-cart." But the legacy he had received could not bear this strain for long, and there came a day when he discovered the exchequer was low, and that something would have to be done. He was level-headed enough to know that an absolutely new field offered him the best chance of success, so breaking up his establishment, and taking leave of his old companions, he went abroad to his eldest brother, who at that time was Deputy Commissioner at Chittagong, in Assam, and he placed him with a tea-planter near there to learn the business. He remained in this occupation some four or five months, but eventually found the monotony of the life even more trying to his restless nature than that on board ship, and gradually becoming convinced that the occupation was not suited to him, he turned his back on tea-planting, and made his way to Calcutta.

The experiences he had undergone now commenced to bear fruit, and on his return home the young man seems to have displayed a little real anxiety as to his future welfare. It became clear to him that the lines he had hitherto followed would not lead to success, or even to mere competence. At this time his second brother, Friend, was house-surgeon at St. Mary's Hospital, and it may have been this fact that suggested to his mind that a medical career was perhaps the one Fate had mapped out for him ; at any rate, he was constantly at the hospital, mixing with the students, among whom were several, such as Dr. Edmund Owen, Dr. George Field, and Dr. Malcolm Morris, who have since become famous in the various branches of the profession. With some of these he formed friendships that lasted as long as life itself. He joined heart and soul in their amusements and games, and those with whom he played at the time are unanimously of the opinion that he was a remarkably clever and capable half-back in Rugby football. But at their work he drew the line. It has been stated that he was a medical student, but such is not the case ; he never was entered on the hospital books. At this period of his life he seemed physically incapable of giving his mind to anything which involved serious thought or responsibility. One of his then comrades, Dr. Edmund Owen, thus speaks of him :—

" He had a fancy for surgery, which, if en

couraged, might have caused him to develop into a dashing, if somewhat reckless, surgeon. But this was not encouraged, though it never entirely left him, inducing him to perform various little operations such as vaccination upon those members of his household and his theatrical friends as would offer themselves as patients.

"He liked also to prescribe medicines to his friends, though there is no evidence to show that these were ever made up. Rather the con-trary seems to be the case, for it is not on record that a death occurred among those for whom he prescribed.

"Sitting in his dressing-room at the Adelphi, observing him 'make up,' I have said to him, 'Billy, you are a marvel! How do you manage to keep your figure and your face so youthful?' His reply was invariably the same. 'Ah, dear boy, I take care of myself.'

"And so he did. He was proud of his clear-cut face and his slim, manly figure, and rightly so.

"There was one thing about Terriss which should be known widely—he was a very careful and abstemious man in his eating and drinking. He had a sort of 'nursery dinner' late in the after- noon, and when his acting was over at night he went home to bed, taking for supper a rice pudding, or something of that sort.

" But whether Terriss was off the stage or on it, whether he was digging in his garden or being falsely accused before a sympathetic Adelphi audience—in short, whatever he was doing, or wherever he happened to be, he was always the same dear breezy fellow, and I loved him."

His idea of a doctor's life, if it ever had been anything more than a passing fancy, faded as quickly as it had sprung into being ; but his com- panionship with the young "meds" provided him with the equally brief career that quickly succeeded it, namely that of engineering. Dr. George P. Field, the present Dean of St. Mary's Hospital Medical School, is happily able to throw some light upon this particular point. He says : " I well re- member his asking me one day, ' How does your brother like engineering ?' and when I said that it just suited him, how he immediately replied,

'It will just suit me.' Next day he was duly apprenticed to be with my brother, and I think at a large premium, to a firm of engineers in Oxford Street. I shall never forget meeting him, shortly afterwards, walking down that same street, in the garb of an engine-driver, with face and hands black, and clothes which had once been white, bedaubed with grease and tar. Engineering amused him for a while, but he soon threw it up, and turned his attention to something else."

It was at this time, just after his engineering proclivities had received their *quietus*, that he participated in a huge joke that brought ridicule on the town of Weston-super-Mare for years afterwards. It is true that at the outset he was an innocent party to it, but directly he saw the way of the wind he entered into the matter heart and soul, and played his part in such a manner as to secure success, as long as the joke lasted. He had been able to render a considerable service to a rich and somewhat eccentric relative of his, and with him and his friend Mr. Graves proceeded to Weston-super-Mare to join a yacht, on board which they were to sail for a pleasure cruise in the Mediterranean. Money was no object with his relative, and they travelled from Town in a special saloon carriage attached to the night mail. But let the adventure be described by the daily *Bristol Times and Mirror* of Wednesday, March 1st, 1865, merely premising that, in view of his sea trip, Lewin had arrayed himself in the uniform he wore during his fortnight's apprenticeship to Messrs. Green & Co.

An Extraordinary Scene at Weston-super Mare.

Weston-super-Mare was yesterday under a strange influence, which made hundreds of the usually exceedingly wide-awake inhabitants the victims of mistaken identity. Early in the morning the startling intelligence was circulated that a Prince of the Royal blood had honoured the town with a visit! At a little before two o'clock yesterday (Tuesday) morning, on the arrival of the London mail at the railway station, the officials, with mingled feelings of astonishment and joy, observed that, attached to the train, was a saloon carriage, approximating in its exterior and interior fittings to the comfortable travelling houses which Royalty uses when on a railway journey.

This carriage had been started with the train from Paddington station, and conveyed a gentleman, his nephew (a lad, apparently about seventeen or eighteen years old), and a neat-looking valet. This was certainly an incident beyond the common run—a phase in the railway officials' existence that undoubtedly does not occur every day. The passengers—who were they? Alighted from the train, the distinguished travellers proceeded at once to the Bath Hotel.

From its being without doubt a Royal train carriage in which the gentleman had arrived, the youngest of the party (the nephew), a good-looking young gentleman, was presumed—nay, stated unhesitatingly—to be no less a personage than His Royal Highness the Prince Alfred. The party went to bed, got up in the ordinary course, and were partaking of breakfast, when, to the extreme surprise of the valet, all sorts of inquiries were made as to the arrival of one of the Royal blood. The valet was astounded, and scarcely knew what reply to make, save to deny that the rumour was true. But this would not satisfy the inquirers, who were determined that a Prince was among them, and would not be convinced of their error. During the morning rounds of one of our principal medical practitioners, he had occasion to call at the hotel to see a former patient. This gentleman had the good fortune to meet the senior of the party whose arrival had created so much excitement, and he was consulted as to what steps had best be taken to abuse the expectant public of their mistake. From that hour the news which before had been confided only to a favoured few spread rapidly over the town, that a member of the Royal Family was staying at the Bath Hotel. The authorities and the public were at once on the *qui vive*. A small list of official personages, including magistrates, police, tradesmen, and members of other portions of the Great Western community, met, we understand, to discuss what shape a demonstration in honour of the Imperial visitors should assume. The doctor recommended that nothing at all should be done, as the occasion did not demand it, and requested that all inquirers should be told that they were entirely misinformed. It was subsequently arranged that, in order to escape further annoyance, the gentlemen should order a carriage to take them to the railway, prior to leaving by the 3.30 p.m. train. This carriage was ordered, and it was hoped that nothing more would be done in the matter; but no, a Royal visitor does not visit Weston-super-Mare every day, and it was too good an opportunity for future distinguishment to be lost. The church bells were set a-ringing in honour of what was everywhere talked of as " the auspicious occasion," and a spirited fly proprietor furnished a wonderful "turn-out"—four spanking grey tits and a resplendent carriage, with two well-dressed postillions. This elaborate vehicle conveyed the distinguished persons to the railway station, the doctor being one of the party. In front of and around the approach to the station was congregated an immense crowd,

the component and not over-select parts of which
immediately surrounded the visitors and pressed
forward to see " the Prince," treading on their
neighbours' toes, elbowing them mercilessly, and
taking particular care of themselves. . . .
Our correspondent was informed that a chemist
of ultra-patriotic feelings forwarded to the Bath
Hotel a bottle of scent for " the Prince," as a
small but sincere mark of esteem, accompanying
the same with an epistle couched in the most
glowing terms, and complimenting His Royal
Highness on his illustrious descent from a long
and royal line of ancestors. When the party left
the Bath Hotel for the railway station, numbers
of people congregated, and in the most respectful
manner bowed them out ; and when going down
the High Street, a shop lad threw into the
carriage another scent bottle, crying with immense
fervour, " Long live Prince Alfred ! "

Lewin long preserved the scent bottle as a me-
mento of the joke, which he was never tired of
relating, and added this further incident, not mentioned in the newspaper report—that, while on

their way to the station, the carriage was stopped, and an enthusiastic lady presented him with a large bouquet, accompanied by a lengthy address, couched in glowing terms.

CHAPTER II

ON AND OFF THE STAGE

HIS pleasure trip over, young Lewin returned to London, and the question of adopting some profession again exercised his mind. He had previous to this frequently taken part in amateur theatricals in various localities, the honour of having been the first to introduce him to the stage being claimed by Dr. George Field when house-surgeon at St. Mary's—so to that institution may be accorded the distinction of being the birthplace of the latent talent which in after years made such a mark in England and America. He says :—

" I used every year, with the assistance of Dr. Milner Moore, now of Coventry, to get up private theatricals, followed by a ball, in aid of the hospital funds, which were always benefited thereby in a sum of from £150 to £180. On one occasion I was the King in *Bombastes Furioso*, and Lewin, an ignominious super, had nought to say but—

> 'What will your Majesty please to wear—
> Or red, blue, green, or white or brown?
> Will you please to look at the bill of fare?'

To which I sternly replied,—

> 'Get out of my sight, or I'll knock you down.'

"Of this his first appearance on any boards Lewin was never tired of talking."

The programme of one of the young actor's early appearances is given opposite, and it is a curious fact that, during the compilation of this book, this illustration came under the notice of a gentleman who was present at the performance, and wrote the notice of it for the *Court Journal*, and he remembered how on this occasion Will Lewin made a slip when, as "Augustus Burr" in *The Porter's Knot*, he returns home to find his father at his old trade; and in answer to Mrs. Burr's inquiry, "Have you seen your father?" he exclaimed in ultra heart-broken tones, "Yes, I have—I have—painfully wheeling a strength too great for his load," and how he very coolly cor-

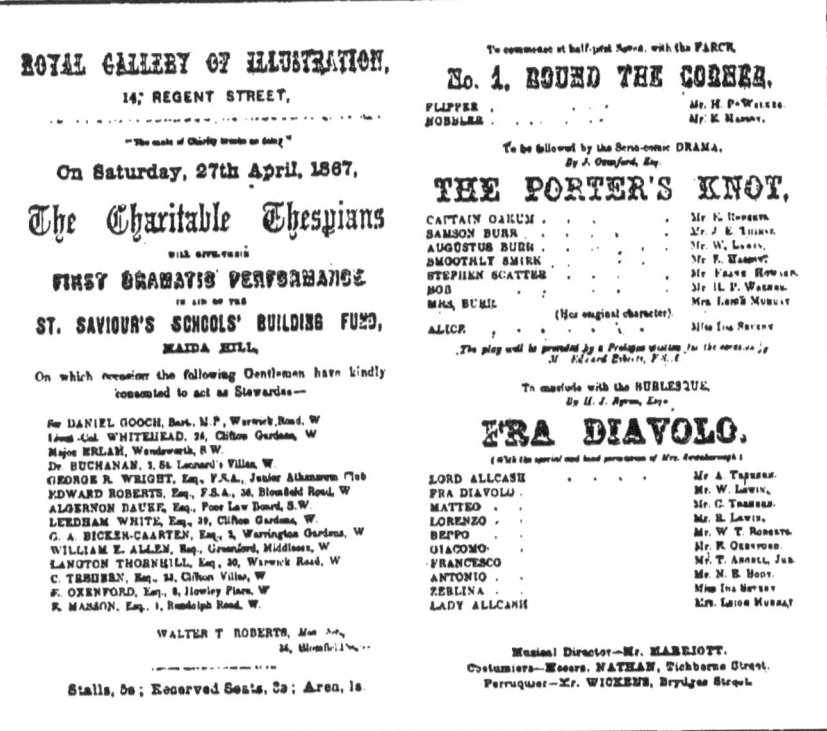

ONE OF HIS FIRST PUBLIC APPEARANCES

(*From* Mrs. CUSHMAN DIGNAM)

rected himself, repeating the sentence, but this time as the author wrote it.

Lewin very soon showed he had something in him, and his appearances were marked by so much success that his services were a good deal sought after in many parts of London, and this it was which probably induced him to take up acting seriously as a means of livelihood.

It was in 1867 that Lewin got his foot on the first step of the theatrical ladder. He was at Birmingham at the time, where the late James Rodgers was playing the leading *rôle* in *Arrah-na-Pogue*, though, owing to his immense proportions, he experienced considerable difficulty in negotiating some of the scenes. Lewin made his acquaintance, and as the result of his expressed determination to go upon the stage, Rodgers deputed him to make up in his own costume, and play his double in the ivy-covered tower scene. This young Lewin did with considerable *éclat*, being honoured with a call. It was during one of those performances for Rodgers that he dropped a valuable diamond out of a ring he was wearing. After the performance he searched high and low for it, but without success. On the following morning one of the working staff restored it to him. Lewin rewarded him, and told him to order a good suit at his tailor's, and he would pay for it.

ON AND OFF THE STAGE

In 1868 he obtained at the Prince of Wales Theatre, Birmingham, his first remunerated engagement (not a very lucrative one, 18s. per week) as "Chouser" in *The Flying Scud*. In this he had a most important speech to deliver, which, in his nervousness, he forgot. He managed to blurt out, "Lady Woodbee has come to town"; and when told by a fellow-actor to go on with his part, he said, "and the rest," and retreated. From that day he was known among his comrades by the sobriquet, "The Rest."

Birmingham did not seem to hold out any great prospect of money-making, and Lewin determined to take the bull by the horns and try his fortune in London. In conjunction with his brother the doctor, and with the help of a directory, he evolved his subsequent stage name of Terriss (the name by which we shall henceforth continue to speak of him), and, thus armed, he set out to interview Mr. Bancroft. The incident of this interview, and the result, may be told in Mr.—now Sir—Squire Bancroft's own words, taken from his Reminiscences.

"During the previous summer we were con-

stantly told by a maidservant that 'a young gentleman had called' who seemed very persistent about
seeing us. One day, on returning from a walk,
the girl informed me that 'the young gentleman'
had brushed past her and walked into our little
drawing-room, where he then was. I joined our
visitor rather angrily, but was soon disarmed by
the frank manner of a very young man, who, within
five minutes, in the course of conversation pointed
to the window of a house opposite, and said,
'That's the room I was born in.' (We then lived
in a little villa in St. John's Wood.) Of course
'the young gentleman' was stage-struck, and
'wanted to go upon the stage,' adding that 'he
was resolved we should give him an engagement.'
His courage and, if I may say it, his cool perseverance both amused and amazed me ; the very
force of his determined manner conquered me, and
the upshot of our interview was that I did engage
him. His name was William Terriss, and 'Lord
Cloudwrays' in *Society* was the part in which
he made his first appearance on a London stage."

It was, of course, at the old Prince of Wales

AT THE AGE OF 22

From a Photo by WINDOW & GROVE

Theatre in Tottenham Street that his *début* took place, and the fact that he was to appear gathered many of his former colleagues to the first night. They distributed themselves over the house, and the entry of their friend was the signal for such an outburst of enthusiasm as almost amounted to a riot, which, instead of furthering the end they had in view, very nearly caused him to lose the position he had obtained. As was only natural, one of his brothers was present to see how he got on, and after the play they met and strolled homeward together. Conscious of the brilliant success he imagined he had achieved, he was constantly expecting his brother's congratulations, but that gentleman was silent on the point until Terriss ventured to ask his opinion. He thereupon whispered in his ear,—

"Chuck it up, dear boy ; you'll never do."

At the Prince of Wales Terriss was really a "walking gentleman," boyish and bright, with a somewhat hurried method of speech, and considerable restlessness of manner. It was during this engagement that he married Miss Isabel

Lewis, who, as Miss Amy Fellowes, had been a member of the Vaudeville company when Montague, Thorne, and James reigned in the little Strand house. The first meeting of the young people took place at Margate, where the attention of the lady was attracted by some of Terriss's swimming feats. The admiration was mutual, and an introduction having taken place, the pair sauntered on the promenade. But it so happened that on this day the lady wished to go back to London by the three o'clock train. This arrangement did not suit Terriss, who was anxious to have her company for a longer time; he left her for a moment and put his watch back a couple of hours. Very shortly after rejoining her she asked him the time, and he replied, "One o'clock." She expressed her surprise that the time had passed so slowly, but on glancing at his watch was convinced. They went for a drive, and had lunch, after which they drove to the station, when by the clock there it was 5.30. The lady declared she had been grossly deceived, but Terriss was able, after a long argument, to make her believe his watch had stopped without his being aware of the fact, and she eventually forgave him.

The marriage took place at Holy Trinity Church, by Portland Road Station, and was a very quiet and unconventional function. Terriss had merely told his brother and his old friend, Mr. Graves, that he was going to be married at such a church, on such a date, and at such a time, and the various parties interested arrived for the most part by 'bus, and in every-day costume. The ceremony was performed, and the happy pair set out for their honeymoon at Richmond on a 'bus.

The part entrusted to him in *Society* was a small one, and as the other artistes included such well-known actors as Hare, Montague, Blakeley, John Clarke, Bancroft, and Montgomery, Terriss had naturally very little chance of shining. It may have been that he felt this, or that, even though he had found an opening in Town, theatrical life did not seem exactly to suit him ; at any rate, there suddenly came another change in his programme, and a wild determination again to try his luck abroad having seized him, he made preparations for a departure to the Falkland Islands, with the view of becoming a sheep farmer.

He and his young wife started from Southampton on a Brazilian mail packet bound for Monte Video, but on reaching that spot they found it in a state of siege. However, they were allowed to land, and reached their hotel, only to be detained there a far longer time than they had anticipated. Their stay was one of anything but pleasure, and both Terriss and his wife regarded themselves as in imminent danger of losing their lives. They had not a single weapon of defence, and in view of the strange commotion, and the determined efforts of the natives to effect an entrance, Terriss could only block up the doorway of their apartment and wait for more quiet times.

Under these exceptionally trying conditions they remained for at least a week, when matters assumed a more peaceful aspect, and they were enabled, and not too soon, to turn their backs upon the place, and in a small coasting steamer, which had previously been Lord Dufferin's yacht, the *Foam*, proceed *en route* for the Falkland Islands.

ON AND OFF THE STAGE

The outward voyage, however, was by no means of a pleasant character. A few days after leaving Monte Video the yacht encountered exceedingly foul weather. A pampero arose, and raged with its accustomed ferocity for nine days, in the midst of which the vessel ran into a British barque ; but the collision was not sufficiently powerful to cut her down.

For five days Mrs. Terriss remained in her bunk, and the crew and passengers every moment felt they were destined for a watery grave.

The vessel was waterlogged, the pumps refused to act, and all hope seemed to be gone. Terriss and his wife at this time had a very anxious talk. The question at issue was whether they should die together ; whether he should first shoot his wife and then himself.

Happily this design was not carried into effect, for Terriss, looking ahead, sighted the desired haven, and hope revived. For the moment Fate seemed to favour them, the pumps again worked, and a speedy termination of their troubles appeared at hand ; but very soon the gale arose once more with increased vigour, and caused the yacht to drift more than two hundred miles out of her proper course.

Terriss now for the first time in his career stood forward as a leader of men. In their dilemma he urged all on board to the greatest exertions. His instructions were obeyed. Again and again he renewed his request to those around him not to lose heart. Signals of distress were hoisted, and in due time the entire crew and passengers were rescued, after having endured keen privations which had almost been their death.

On landing at the Falkland Islands Terriss and his wife received quite a royal greeting. Especially was this the case with Mrs. Terriss, who was the first white lady to step upon the shore. In honour of this event the natives crowned her with tufts of woven grass, and declared her queen, if not of the island, " of their hearts."

Having settled at Stanley, Terriss entered into partnership with Captain Pack in the business of sheep farming, and a very extensive trade they did. While in pursuit of his business Mrs. Terriss was of necessity left a great deal to her own resources, in the little cottage which they made their home. Here, surrounded by a goodly number of the native population, she became intensely nervous. The people forced their attentions upon her, and honoured her in such a way as to be distasteful to her. Her husband was apprised of this on more than one occasion, and, while sympathizing with her in her loneliness, he endeavoured to impress upon her that these overtures were made out of the kindest of motives. She failed to appreciate his remarks, and asked him to pitch his tent elsewhere, if possible somewhere nearer home, and amid more congenial surroundings.

Terriss was next found training wild horses. Dressed in a most picturesque costume, he got on famously, not only with the horses, but also with the men whom he employed. He manipulated the lasso with much dexterity, and was specially marked out as an expert in the craft. One particular animal was voted untameable. Terriss, however, mastered him, but not without experiencing considerable difficulty. His success or ardour declined by degrees, and he gave up the game. From taming wild animals he tried his hand in the same direction with wild fowl. In this he was not encouraged by success, although he made the most elaborate arrangements in order to adequately carry out his scheme ; so he gave up the experiment, and filled up his time by making little trips of discovery in the vicinity of his settlement.

About this time H.M.S. *Speedwell* put into the harbour. Terriss, " got up " as a lieutenant, paid the captain a visit, and led him to believe he was somebody of great importance. He related the fact that his wife, on her landing, had been crowned queen of the island ; and that being the case, he argued, he must be the king. The story was evidently believed by the captain, as the *Speedwell*, on leaving the harbour, dipped her flag thrice and fired her guns in honour of the pair. In response Terriss made for his cottage, which stood in an elevated position hard by, and, having secured a red silk handkerchief to a broom handle, got on the roof, waved his " flag " three times, and then fastened the staff to the chimney-pot.

ON AND OFF THE STAGE

For the purpose of making observations, Terriss built a punt, which to his mind appeared seaworthy. Under ordinary circumstances perhaps he was right, but on one occasion she was put to a very severe test. All went well enough until out in the open sea, when a gale arose and knocked her timbers asunder, leaving her skipper to the mercy of the waves. He, however, managed to reach the shore, and this experience put an end to any similar excursions in the future.

Before making that adventurous journey he had planted in his garden a number of radishes, and, in order adequately to describe the force of this gale, Terriss told his friends that some of the plants were blown far, far away. One of these, he declared, was found on the rigging of a ship anchored at the distance of two miles.

Terriss tarried at the little station for about twelve months, when he and his wife returned to the settlement "Stanley," where his daughter was born. The ceremony attending the christening of the child was one of pomp and grandeur. The sponsors were the governor of the islands (Colonel

D'Arcy) and his wife, with whom the Terriss's were on the closest terms of friendship.

He now earnestly spoke of his desire to return to England, and notwithstanding the warm entreaties of the governor and the numerous friends he had made on the island, he determined to take his departure at once. Owing to the very heavy harbour dues, a first-class vessel seldom came into that port. He refused to wait for the arrival of the next, and so booked passages on a whaler hailing from Honolulu, which a Swedish captain had been sent out to purchase.

Terriss, his wife and the child, who was but a fortnight old, were taken alongside the whaler on the governor's yacht. The crew of the homeward-bound vessel was a mixed lot, and the captain turned out to be a most undesirable fellow. In consequence of this officer having reduced the allowance of the crew to three biscuits and a pint of water a day, mutiny broke out among them. For some reason the men rallied round Terriss, and made him their captain *pro tem.*, ordering the mate to render him every possible assistance. The course thus adopted increased the enmity of the captain towards the crew, and also embittered him against the three passengers to such an extent that he had recourse to most extreme measures regarding their food.

Naturally Terriss would not allow such a state of things to go on. He stoutly protested against this injustice, and declared that he would force open the provision locker and dole out eatables as they were required. He was, however, prevented from carrying out his purpose to the fullest extent, and seeing that the health of his wife and baby was suffering from the want of proper and regular meals, he was, in order to obtain sufficient food, obliged to kill a pet goat which the governor had given him to provide milk on the voyage.

Upon learning what had been done, the captain became almost frantic, and threatened to take the carcass from him. Overhearing the altercation between the two, Mrs. Terriss intervened, and succeeded in pacifying the master. Terriss was highly amused at the wrangle, and afterwards, by way of jest, promised to give the captain the kidneys.

From this time both the quantity and quality of the provisions improved all round, and upon the captain again taking command, matters went on more smoothly and pleasantly ; but the whole voyage was of a most dull and dreary character, extending over four months, and the passengers arrived at Falmouth more dead than alive.

CHAPTER III

AT LEXINGTON, KENTUCKY

IN September, 1871, having settled in a pleasantly situated cottage at Barnes, Terriss obtained an engagement at Drury Lane, and appeared as " Robin Hood " in Mr. Andrew Halliday's drama *Rebecca*, and after that as " Malcolm Græme" in *The Lady of the Lake*, Mr. James Fernandez being " Fitz James." It was not until this engagement that he began to be regarded as a coming "juvenile lead" of very high attainments. Mr. G. R. Sims thus writes of him at that time :—

" My earliest reminiscences of William Terriss carry me back to the early seventies. In a queer little house in Holywell Street a few theatrical and newspaper men had started a club. It has long since disappeared, but it was famous in its day. The old Unity Club flourished in the palmy days of the Strand Theatre, and the Swanboroughs were

47

its constant patrons. At the Unity Club day after day a few actors and journalists met and dined together at three o'clock. Among the men who dined frequently were Edward and Arthur Swanborough, David James, Thomas Thorne, Walter Joyce, H. B. Farnie, George Honey, George Barratt, James Albery, Harry Leigh, and William Terriss. Terriss, when I first met him at the Unity, was playing at Drury Lane in *The Lady of the Lake.* In those days Terriss was looked upon as a promising young actor. He was immensely popular with all of us, and it was a rare thing to go to the Unity in the afternoon and not find young Terriss the life and soul of a merry little party. We all prophesied that he had a great future before him, and our prophecy was speedily fulfilled. Important engagements were offered to him at the leading West-End houses, and he became a great London favourite."

But by-and-by his restless, roving spirit once more asserted itself, and again throwing his chance of success on the stage aside, he arranged to join one of his old schoolfellows, Mr. Percy Tattersall, nephew of the head of the firm at Knightsbridge, in a horse-breeding venture at Lexington, Kentucky. It was a sudden impulse, and little time was spent in consideration. Mrs. Terriss was asked to pack up what goods and chattels they would require on the voyage and afterwards, and once more to become a traveller. She naturally felt loth to leave her newly-made home, but having implicit faith in her husband she resigned herself, and they and their daughter set off together.

Arriving at Lexington in due course, safe and sound, they failed to discover the golden streets, picturesque villas, and love-birds so much talked of before they left England, but instead had to encounter the greatest irregularity, rudeness, and confusion. They made their abode in a wooden shanty, which consisted of three small rooms, and a yard in which the cooking operations were carried on ; a somewhat spacious tree - trunk served as a cooking-range. This yard was the rendezvous of rats, and it can be readily imagined with what difficulty the most important domestic offices were carried out. Mrs. Terriss, who had so far displayed much heroism, was determined not to show the white feather now. Nor did she, but pluckily faced and conquered all the many difficulties by which she was surrounded.

Brimful of the delights and anticipations of his new vocation, Terriss rose with studied punctuality at five o'clock each morning, and spent the first two or three hours in horse-doctoring. He was in his element again, but before very long his ardour began to wane, this time principally by reason of his vanishing capital, and his thoughts once more reverted to the stage, and to the friends he had left behind him in England.

Speaking some years afterwards of his past experiences, he mentioned an incident which took place at this time, and it may not be uninteresting to record his words. He said :—

" I have been knocking about the world for over twenty-five years, as most people know, and although I am simply known as an actor, I have by turns been a midshipman, tea-planter, engineer, sheep-farmer, and horse-breeder, and in pursuit of these occupations I have naturally visited all sorts and conditions of places, hobnobbed with every kind of queer folk, and found myself in extremely queer predicaments.

"I have been baked by tropical suns, drenched and frozen by icy-cold waves, parched with thirst, devoured by hunger, placed in peril of my life scores of times, and in turns kindly and unkindly treated by the people with whom I have come in contact; but I have always recognised the fact that life is too short to bear enmities : I have never lost a friend.

"Owing, I suppose, to a certain waywardness of disposition, and a dislike of staying in one place or doing one thing for any length of time, I have roamed perhaps more than I should have done. All my ventures, other than those pertaining to the stage, have met with little or no success. I have, therefore, known what it is to want a friend with a warm heart and a ready hand.

"But I am now going to tell you a tale about a friend *not* of this sort. He was one of those kind-hearted individuals who never allow themselves to lose faith in human nature, and of whom, alas! the world possesses far too few.

"In 1871 I went to Kentucky, accompanied by my young wife and daughter, Ellaline, who was at the time twelve months old. I soon found that the road which I had been led to believe was paved with the 'almighty dollar' was a thoroughfare where this coin was unknown, at any rate to me.

"After I had, in conjunction with Mr. Tattersall, expended all my money on horse-breeding, I found myself absolutely stranded and penniless, so decided to return to England, and follow once more in the footsteps of Thespis.

"And then came the question, 'How am I to get home?' Fortunately, on my arrival, I joined the Masonic lodge at the place, of which the worshipful master was a Mr. Oliver, who was a large coachbuilder of Lexington. To him I narrated my misfortunes. With the courtesy and good fellowship which ever characterizes the brotherhood, he then and there lent me what I asked, and in giving me the money he said, 'Pay me

back when you can, my boy. God speed and
God bless you ! '

" I accepted the help gratefully, and, travelling
steerage, returned to England. I need hardly
say I remitted him the amount before I had been
at home twenty-four hours, at the same time
thanking him very heartily for his generous kindness."

It may be added that, on the way home, Terriss
became such a favourite with the saloon passengers
that he spent most of his time in their company,
and after dining with them he would invariably
bring to the steerage passengers a host of dainty
morsels. His kindness to them was much appreciated, and on leaving the ship he was the recipient
of many good wishes from all those whom he had
befriended.

During one of his professional visits to America,
many years afterwards, he happened to be playing
within a hundred miles of Lexington, and, taking
an early train one Sunday morning, he entered that
beautiful city as the church bells were ringing for
afternoon service.

"Lighting my pipe," he said, "I leisurely strolled up to the well-remembered spot, and as I approached Mr. Oliver's house [it will be remembered that Mr. Oliver was the gentleman who had befriended him in a moment of need] I noticed that the blinds were closely drawn, and that everywhere were manifestations of mourning.

"I knocked at the door, and an elderly lady opened it. I inquired if Mr. Oliver, the coach-builder, were within. Her eyes moistened, and in tremulous tones she told me that only the day previously had he been laid to rest in 'God's Acre.'

"The lady was his wife. I recalled the circumstances of my former visit to the house, and she recognised me. A few words of kindly sympathy, a pressure of the hand that spoke more than any words could have done, and I departed, happy to think that I had done what I thought to be a duty to a benefactor, but regretful that I had been too late to clasp once more that hand which had been held out to me in my hour of trouble.

"And, as I walked back to the roadside station,

AT LEXINGTON, KENTUCKY

I could not refrain from repeating those beautiful words of Longfellow, which seemed to me to have been written specially for such occasions as this :—

" 'Ships that pass in the night, and speak each other in passing,
  Only a signal shown and a distant voice in the darkness ;
  So in the ocean of life we pass and speak one another,
  Only a look and a voice, then darkness again and silence.' "

CHAPTER IV

TO ONE THING CONSTANT

ONCE more safe back in England, the wandering, unrestful spirit of Terriss seems to have died out of him, and he settled down to work in earnest, having found, and from that time keeping to, his real vocation, which was that of an actor. By this time he had probably learnt that a Jack of all trades and master of none was not a very lucrative employment, and besides this he was married and had a family, so that the free, harum-scarum, adventurous, and almost hand-to-mouth life he had lived up till this time could not be followed so easily. He now had others beside himself to think of and to work for.

It was in 1873 that he made his third attack on the stage, and from this moment his success in life may be said to date. He obtained an engagement at the Strand, and appeared as " Doricourt " in *The*

AT THE AGE OF 26
From a Photo by WINDOW & GROVE

Belle's Stratagem, which ran for 250 consecutive
nights. The success he obtained furnished the
encouragement which had hitherto been lacking,
and fortified him in his determination to win a name
as an actor. He went to work with a will, and left
no stone (or study) unturned that might assist him
in attaining his ambitious goal. Those who witnessed his early appearances in London may
doubtless remember that although he evinced great
promise, he did not possess that ringing and beautifully balanced delivery which afterwards proved of
so much service to him. He himself was evidently
aware of this deficiency, for he commenced studying
declamation carefully, and in secret, being not
unmindful of the sage advice given him by many a
veteran elocutionist, who liked "the lively young
spark," and wished him well. With some, it is
probable that such advice would have influenced
the recipient in such a way as to lead him to cling
to certain traditions and mannerisms even then
expiring ; but Terriss had his head screwed on the
right way, and was shrewd enough to select from
these counsels all that might be useful to him in the

new era, while retaining most of his own more up-to-date methods and ideas.

On the conclusion of his Strand engagement he returned to Drury Lane, to appear as "Sir Kenneth" in *Richard Cœur de Lion*, and on its withdrawal Miss Wallis found in him a picturesque "Romeo" to her "Juliet."

During the long run of Dion Boucicault's third great Irish play of *The Shaughraun* (the *Colleen Bawn* and *Arrah-na-Pogue* being the first two of the trio), he was "Captain Molyneux," both at Drury Lane and the Aldephi, to which house it was transferred; and it was this character which suggested to the late Henry S. Leigh a charming set of verses, in which "pretty Miss" from the country, seeing Molyneux from her seat in the pit, is moved to a confession of love for the handsome officer, and of jealousy of fortunate Claire. Poor country miss ! Charming, darling Molyneux can never be hers, he is not even Claire's. Says the culprit himself in the envoy,—

> "A thousand darlings round me seek
> For one sweet smile; but I'll be true
> To Chatterton's twelve pounds a week,
> My kids, and Mrs. Molyneux."

"ROMEO" IN *ROMEO AND JULIET*

From a Photo by W. & D. Downey

TO ONE THING CONSTANT

One of the actor's early engagements was to play the "Brigand" in a certain piece, of the blood-and-thunder type, at Astley's Theatre. In one of the scenes the "Brigand" appeared with his steed "Teddy." In this, having finished with the animal, it was his duty to exclaim, "Get thee to the mountains"; and at the sound of these words "Teddy" would move across the stage and exit. Terriss had got accustomed to "Teddy"; but unfortunately just before one of the performances the animal departed this life, and the management hired one of his species from the stables of the Omnibus Company which were hard by. Every available moment before the show was utilised in rehearsal, but little satisfaction could be got out of Teddy II. He was, however, led on to the stage at the proper time. Terriss gave forth the usual exhortation, and the scene-shifter held out, as an inducement to the beast to go in his direction, a handful of provender or a bunch of carrots. He would not, however, budge an inch. The words were repeated, and his tail twisted, but to no avail. Then what turned out to be a happy idea dawned upon the actor. He remembered that he was dealing with a 'bus horse, and that the conductor's signal to move on was invariably a few sharp stamps on the footboard. With considerable emphasis he again repeated the sentence, and imitated the action of the conductor on the boards, and this had the desired effect.

Both at the Adelphi and the Princess's he appeared in several revivals, and once more returning to The Lane, was selected for "Julian" in Mr. Wills's version of *Peveril of the Peak*.

It was in the year 1874 or 1875 that he made a success in the title *rôle* of "Nicholas Nickleby" at the Adelphi, when the late Miss Lydia Foote appeared as "Smike" and the late John Clarke as "Squeers." In 1876 he appeared as "Beamish MacCoul" in J. C. Williamson's revival of *Arrah-na-Pogue*, which will be remembered as the first play in which he trod the boards professionally, playing double to the late James Rodgers as the hero in the tower scene at the Prince of Wales, Birmingham.

He was the "Earl of Leicester" in the revival of *Amy Robsart*, at Drury Lane, in 1877. But it was on the 30th March, 1878, at the Old Court

"'SQUIRE THORNHILL" IN GRACE
From a Photo by W. & D. DOWNEY

Theatre, that he first represented one of those characters by which he will be more generally remembered, viz. "Squire Thornhill," in W. G. Wills's play of *Olivia*. Associated with him was Ellen Terry in the title *rôle*, and Herman Vezin as "Dr. Primrose." In this year he was also "Fawley Denham" in *The Crisis*, by Albery, "Captain Absolute" in *The Rivals*, and "Sydney Sefton" in *Conscience Money*, by the late H. J. Byron.

A lady journalist thus writes of him about this time: "But I must not allow myself to be drawn into reminiscences, for here — I mean where Terriss is—is a matter more attractive. I wonder if you have heard much of this charming *jeune premier* who plays quite too bewitchingly, and in a series of bows, the part of 'Captain Absolute.' It is difficult to define the winning personality of this well-pleasing lad. But I think in the first place that he must have provided himself with a newly-invented patent hinged back, which enables him to personify the very embodiment of gentlemanly grace. It is in the true spirit of Sheridan's gallant day, this facile bowing, and is relieved by a proud, sweet, manly bearing, unmistakably indicative of the well-born youth of noble England. This, with his languid eye and *expirante* manner, makes him the predestine hero of many a gentle heart's romance ; it is inevitable. Repudiating any spark of sentimentality in my own admiration of him, do you think—but perhaps I'd better put it in confidence—do you think that if a highly moral American lady like myself, wife of an officer in the Civil Service of the United States Government, above suspicion of folly in every way, and quite unacquainted personally with the young actor, were to quietly kiss him the next time she meets him in the street, it would be considered at all peculiar ? Well, then, whatever is he so pretty for ? *C'est de sa faute, aussi."*

1879 found him at the St. James's, scoring largely as " Jack Gambier " in *The Queen's Shilling*, " Count de la Roque " in *Monsieur le Duc*, and also in *Still Waters run Deep.*

In this year also he was playing " Romeo " to the " Juliet " of the late Miss Neilson, and being his first appearance with her in the part, he wished to make the best impression he could, and attended the dress rehearsal fully equipped with a dagger and a Damascus blade, sharp as a razor. He was about to begin the duel with "Mercutio," when Miss Neilson stopped him, and entreated him not to proceed further save with a blunt weapon. He followed her advice, but a few years later he evidently forgot her counsel, and was wounded when playing the same part with Miss Mary Anderson, for in falling upon the dagger it pierced his side.

On 20th September, 1880, he commenced his long connection with the Lyceum Theatre, playing "M. de Chateau Renaud" in *The Corsican Brothers.* This ran till 3rd January, 1881, when *The Cup,* by Alfred, first Lord Tennyson, was produced, and in this Terriss was "Sinnatus." On 16th April *The Belle's Stratagem* was mounted, and he was now seen as "Flutter," a part which was always assigned to him in the various later revivals of the play. On the 18th May in the same year commenced the famous series of performances of *Othello,* a series unexampled in the history of the

stage, seeing that the parts of "Othello" and
"Iago" were alternated each week by Edwin
Booth and Henry Irving. In this Terriss played
"Cassio." The prices of the stalls were raised to
two guineas, and fabulous sums were given for
boxes to witness the greatest tragedians of the
sister countries unselfishly and harmoniously playing on the same stage. *Othello* was only played
three evenings a week, the remaining three being
filled by the regular company in *The Cup* and
The Belle's Stratagem.

In the revivals with which the lessee of the
Lyceum always brings his season to a close, Terriss
appeared as "Laertes" in *Hamlet*, "Christian" in
The Bells, "Bassanio" in *The Merchant of Venice*,
and "Richard Houseman" in *Eugene Aram.*

Boxing Day of the same year saw him still at
the Lyceum, personating "Jack Wyatt" in James
Albery's *Two Roses*, a revival which served to
introduce George Alexander to a London audience
as "Caleb Deecie." He also played "Viscount de
Ligny" in Planché's *Captain of the Watch.* On
8th March, 1882, *Romeo and Juliet* was produced,

"MERCUTIO" IN *ROMEO AND JULIET*
From a Photo by W. & D. DOWNEY

and ran to the end of that season, and well into the autumn one. In this Terriss was "Mercutio," giving an admirable, and even a perfect, interpretation. No praise was too high for his death scene ; he sank to the real level of nature, and died with the airs and words with which Mercutio—Shakespeare's Mercutio—should pass from the world. He was now making real headway in his profession, and about this time a critic wrote of him : "It is difficult to imagine an improvement more rapid or more distinct than that of the young actor since he quitted melodrama for comedy."

It was during this year that, while playing in Dublin, and lodging with Mr. Tyars, of the Lyceum, in a small inn on the outskirts of the city, he found out that a section of the "Invincibles" held their meetings in a room in the house. This knowledge put an idea into his head, and one evening he made his way alone into the room, and marching boldly up to the table, brought his hand down upon it sharply, at the same time exclaiming in a tone of authority, "In the name of the Queen this meeting is dissolved." This statement, delivered by a perfect stranger in the stronghold of treachery, seemed to paralyse the conspirators present ; they gazed at him in silent astonishment, but did not offer to move. Seeing this, Terriss repeated the assertion with more emphasis than before, and this time it had a curious effect, for the whole of those present silently rose, and taking their hats, filed out of the room, leaving the dare-devil originator of the joke unharmed, to make his peace with the terrified landlord, who declared he would be simply ruined through the occurrence.

Another long run commenced on the 11th October, 1882, when in *Much Ado about Nothing* Terriss took the part of " Don Pedro," and played it till the piece was withdrawn, to make way for the usual series of short revivals which brought the season to a conclusion in July, 1883. Among these he appeared as "Courriol" in *The Lyons Mail,* " Charles " in *Robert Macaire,* " Earl of Moray " in *Charles I.,* and the " Duke de Nemours " in *Louis XI.*

In the autumn of this year he went with the Lyceum company on their first American tour,

"DON PEDRO" IN *MUCH ADO ABOUT NOTHING*
From a Photo by W. & D. DOWNEY

"EARL OF MORAY" IN *CHARLES I*

From a Photo by W. & D. DOWNEY

which commenced on 19th October, 1883, and lasted
until 26th April, 1884, during which they played
most, if not all, of their London successes. It was
on the outward voyage in the *City of Rome* that
a rather bragging man, seeing so many landlubbers
present not clad like himself in yachting rig, pulled
out a ten-pound note, and offered to wager it that
there was not one of the passengers who would
take his cap off the top of the mast. Terriss instantly covered the note, and throwing off his coat
and tightening his belt, said, "Done! Up with
you, and put it on ; I will follow, and take it off."
The offer was withdrawn.

During the tour several well-known members
of the company joined in an entertainment given
at Chickering Hall. It was a great success, and
the rare talent exhibited won unlimited applause.
Terriss's share consisted of recitations, among
which may be mentioned Queen Mab's speech,
The Wreck of the Hesperus, and *The Life Boat*.

While on this tour the company was rehearsing
The Two Roses on the stage of a New York
theatre, Terriss playing the difficult part of "Jack

79

Wyatt." Irving was sitting on the stage, watching the performance. As on its conclusion he found no fault, Terriss ventured to go up to him with a " Well, governor ; will that do ? " and a sort of air as if he expected a compliment. Irving quietly wiped his glasses, as his habit is, and replied, " Yes, very good ; but not a d——d bit like it."

But the chief result of this visit to America, as far as the general public is concerned, was the introduction to London by Terriss of the famous Daly company, who since that time have continued to pay us visits at varying intervals, and are now so much at home here that they possess a theatre of their own.

In the summer of this year Terriss became leading man to Miss Mary Anderson during her visit, playing in *Pygmalion and Galatea, The Hunchback*, and as " Romeo " to her " Juliet." In connection with this it was remarked that none remembered a Romeo who in years and good looks was so likely to take captive the heart of Juliet at first sight. There had been Romeos of the namby-pamby order, but there was nothing of the kind about

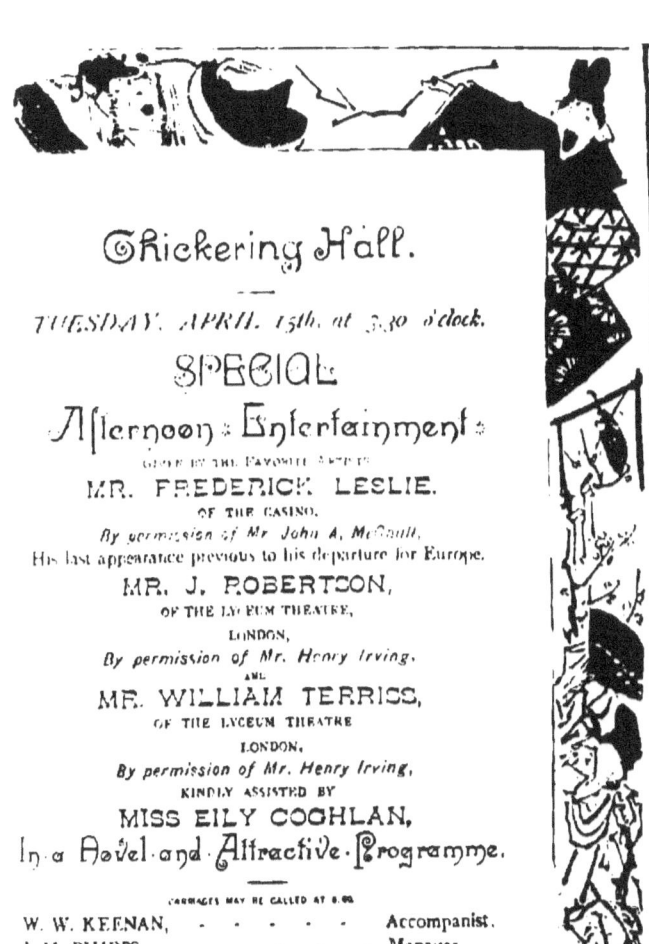

Chickering Hall.

TUESDAY, APRIL. 15th, at 3.30 o'clock.

SPECIAL

Afternoon · Entertainment ·

GIVEN BY THE FAVORITE ARTISTS

MR. FREDERICK LESLIE.
OF THE CASINO.
By permission of Mr John A. McCaull.
His last appearance previous to his departure for Europe.

MR. J. ROBERTSON,
OF THE LYCEUM THEATRE,
LONDON,
By permission of Mr. Henry Irving.
AND

MR. WILLIAM TERRISS,
OF THE LYCEUM THEATRE
LONDON,
By permission of Mr. Henry Irving,
KINDLY ASSISTED BY

MISS EILY COGHLAN,
In a Novel · and · Attractive · Programme.

CARRIAGES MAY BE CALLED AT 6.00

W. W. KEENAN, - - - - - - Accompanist.
J. H. PHIPPS, - - - - - - Manager.

Terriss. His Romeo, although in love, could be manly as well as tender. He played the balcony scene with wonderful fervour; he took the measure of his new-made grave in a way that for once did not provoke a smile at Romeo's expense; he talked to the apothecary like a desperate lover who was very much in earnest, and he went through the business of the final sorrowful scene with splendid impressiveness. He, however, made a great hit in the encounter with Tybalt after Mercutio's death :—

> "Alive! in triumph! and Mercutio slain;
> Away to heaven, respective lenity,
> And fire-eyed fury be my conduct now!
> Now, Tybalt, take the villain back again,
> That late thou gav'st me; for Mercutio's soul
> Is but a little way above our heads,
> Staying for thine to keep him company;
> Either thou, or I, or both, must go with him."

This passage Terriss delivered with electrical force, and his elocutionary skill, coupled with the grandeur of the subsequent onslaught, was fairly irresistible.

When Irving played the part so successfully, Terriss as the "Mercutio" has already been referred to. Every one was compelled to give him commendation. When he represented "Romeo" the commendation was not less hearty, for it was an impersonation of the very highest merits, and one which added greatly to the popular actor's already high reputation.

On 27th May, 1885, *Olivia*, by W. C. Wills, was revived, and ran into the autumn season, Terriss and Miss Ellen Terry taking their old characters, while Henry Irving chose that of " Dr. Primrose." In writing of this revival, a critic says :—

" In the suggestive acting of Terriss as 'Squire Thornhill,' and of Miss Ellen Terry in the title *rôle*, there was such a grasp of meaning and wealth of variety that it was said the audience anticipated what was to follow. Clear in voice and distinct in utterance, he never lost sight of one essential consideration ; viz., that although Squire Thornhill was morally contemptible, he was by birth, education, and position a gentleman.

" Stage villains at times come to mean those who are not only morally, but also physically contemptible ; yet had Thornhill been of this pattern he

"SQUIRE THORNHILL" IN *OLIVIA*

From a Photo by WINDOW & GROVE

would never have been loved by Olivia. It was a most difficult part to play, and it was grasped from first to last with singular intelligence, a bold front, and subtle meaning."

On the first night of *Olivia*, at the close of the second act, Terriss did not take a call, and the general audience quietly accepted his refusal. Not so an infatuated young miss in the dress circle. Finding the applause had died away, and her favourite would not exhibit his goodly presence before the curtain, she rose from her seat, and, almost choking with excitement, and clapping her hands wildly, cried, " Ter—rr—iss ! Terriss—ss !" She repeated her obvious indiscretion at the final descent of the curtain.

He next made a move to the Adelphi, where he opened at Christmas, 1885, as " Lieutenant David Kingsley " in *Harbour Lights*, by G. R. Sims and Henry Pettit—a piece that ran without interruption for 513 nights. A well-known critic thus happily describes the impression made upon the vast audience, which nightly crowded the theatre, by the most perfect impersonation of a British sailor

that the stage has ever seen since the days of
J. P. Cooke :—

" The acting of the new play is as good as
it well could be. As ' David Kingsley,' Mr.
William Terriss has a part after his own
heart. He does not act; he is the handsome,
frank sailor whose joyous laugh, bright eye, and
sturdy, ringing voice brings life and hope into the
darkest hour. The fine presence, boyish handsome
face, and free fearless gestures, suit the *rôle* to
perfection ; and in the pretty apostrophe to the
bright eyes of his sweetheart—the ' Harbour
Lights ' that have shone so steadily for him in
storm and darkness—and in the fanciful little ' ring
speech '—' Little ring, I've looked at you, and
you've bidden me hope during many a long, dark
watch at sea. Now we're home again, little ring,
and we're going to part. Somebody else is going
to have you, and to keep you for ever ; but you'll
make Dave Kingsley's sweetheart Dave Kingsley's
wife '—his masterly elocution was of the greatest
service. I have seen Terriss in many parts, but
in none that has left so pleasant and bright a

DAVID KINGSLEY IN _____

From a Photo W. & D. D...y

memory as handsome, manly David Kingsley."

One of the authors of the play thus writes of it and its hero :—

"Its long and lasting popularity was largely due to the buoyant breeziness of Terriss's young naval officer. His portrait in uniform appeared in every shop window, and men and women alike spoke rapturously of him, and hailed him as the ideal hero of melodrama. In 1886 his photograph as 'David Kingsley' was even issued as a Christmas card. In private life Terriss spoke and bore himself very much as he did upon the stage. His frank, buoyant manner and his cheery style of address earned for him the title of 'Breezy Bill'; and his breeziness was not assumed, but was natural to the man. Downright, hearty, outspoken, and independent, William Terriss was invariably amiable ; and even at that trying time to actors and authors alike, the last rehearsals, he always kept his temper and his cheerfulness."

It was during the run of *Harbour Lights* that a fairy-looking, precocious little thing one night attracted much attention. During a short lull in one of the scenes she startled all around her by exclaiming, " Wal, I'm clean mashed on that Mr. Terriss."

Following *The Harbour Lights* came *The Bells of Haselmere*, and in this he represented the hero, "Frank Beresford," winning for himself the honours of the run among the actors. The open, engaging sympathy of the young Squire was happily rendered at his hands; frankness and courage in his every action and tone. It was, however, in the scene in which the fugitive struggles against death in the tangled cane-brake that the artist rose to the highest level of dramatic power. Weary and faint, fighting for life, sustained by the hope of restoration to his love in England, Terriss held the audience in silent admiration at the striking exhibition of his skill.

In *The Silver Falls*, which was afterwards given, Terriss played the hero with his accustomed vigour and conviction. Honour, courage, truth, and all the higher moral sentiments found in him a fearless and uncompromising champion ; and he had the satisfaction of feeling that, despite the

"FRANK BERESFORD" IN *THE BELLS OF HASELMERE*

From a Photo by WINDOW & GROVE

"JACK MEDWAY" IN *THE UNION JACK*

From a Photo by WINDOW & GROVE

adoption by the authors of an unconventional story, his career remained what it had already been in Adelphi melodrama, a shining axiom that honesty is the best policy.

On the reopening of the Adelphi after restoration, July 21st, 1888, *The Union Jack* was produced. Into his character of "Jack Medway," who wore the smart uniform of a petty officer in the navy, Terriss threw extraordinary power ; "the true breath of passion breathed into the play, enabling him to grip the house, so to speak, by the throat. The grace and dignity with which he wore his simple uniform, the resonant effect of his mellow tones, and the bright intelligence of his piercing glance, won for him half the battle of success. And the triumph was grand and cumulative. The truth and delicacy of his scenes with Miss Millward in the first act of the play, the simple chivalry of his behaviour, and the suggestion of just germinating affection in his voice, were admirable enough. But Terriss rose beyond the region of melodrama in the scene outside the cottage, where Rose Medway confesses to her brother the sad secret of her fall. Here his acting was truly elevated. His agonized start, as if physically wounded, as the terrible truth struck home, the manly recoil after the momentary collapse, the bitterness of the strong man's supposed grief, were all admirably depicted."

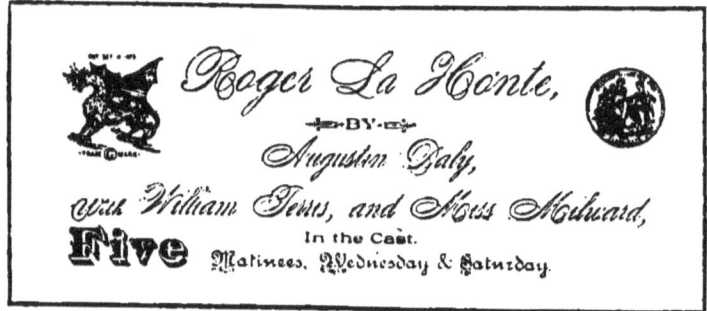

A SOUVENIR

Following this, Terriss, in conjunction with his old artistic ally, Miss Jessie Millward, paid a professional visit to the States in 1889–90, appearing in *Othello*, *Frou Frou*, *The Marble Heart*, *The Lady of Lyons*, *Ingomar*, and last, but not least, in *Roger la Honte*, better known to us in England by the name of *A Man's Shadow*. The general American idea of the piece was that it was a strong play of popular interest, and one that

98

AN AMERICAN PLAYBILL

■

had all the elements requisite for securing a gratify-
ing profit to its owners. It was a decided success,
viewed from the standpoint of popular melodrama.
And, referring to Terris, it was said that "of the
picturesque, swinging elocutionary type of the
romantic actor he was particularly effective. He
never pained his audience. He showed much re-
finement of method, and his work was indeed high
class. As 'Laroque' he was graceful and easy
in his movements, his bearing was manly, and his
face was the index of honour and high principle.
As 'Luversan,' an instant later, his features bore
the impress of recklessness, dissipation, and hate."

At the conclusion of this tour he returned to
the Adelphi for the revival of *The Harbour
Lights*, and then once more found himself at the
Lyceum, engaged for "Hayston of Bucklaw," in
Herman Merivale's adaptation of *Ravenswood*,
with which the season commenced on 20th September, 1890. This character he played exactly
in the right spirit, assertive, but never vulgar;
domineering, but never loud; conceited, but never
foppish. The play required all the relief possible,

and Terriss provided the welcome tone of change from persistent gloom. On 5th January, 1891, *Much Ado about Nothing* was revived; and the Lyceum company, released from the sombre *Ravenswood*, which had fallen somewhat short of the hundred representations deemed in days of long runs the minimum test of a decided success, returned to the bright and merry scenes in Leonato's house and by the blue waters of the Bay of Messina with a manifest zest. Henry Irving appeared as "Benedick," and gave, not the restless Benedick of the Lewis tradition, nor the moody, saturnine Benedick which old lovers of Macready were accustomed to, but the sprightly, courteous, quick-witted gentleman, whose intellectual pride and sensitiveness to ridicule alone delay the manifestation of love for "Dear Lady Disdain," which holds him captive in the end. Miss Ellen Terry, as "Beatrice," was assuredly never brighter or fresher in her wilful moods, nor more sweet and womanly in her more tender movements, than as she now revealed herself to the never-failing delight of the spectators.

"HAYSTON OF BUCKLAW" IN *RAVENSWOOD*

From a Photo by WINDOW & GROVE

"CLAUDIO" IN *MUCH ADO ABOUT NOTHING*

From a Photo by WINDOW & GROVE

TO ONE THING CONSTANT

Terriss lent the support of his noble bearing and excellent elocution to the part of "Claudio." In this he looked handsomer than ever in a most becoming costume. It will be remembered that in the original production he was "Don Pedro," but his "Claudio" was even more admired. His share of the banter of Benedick, and of the trick by which he is caught in Cupid's net, was lightly and effectively done ; and he was magnificently in earnest in the scene at the altar, where Claudio rejects his bride and denounces her as a wanton.

On 2nd June, 1891, he appeared for the first time for a good many years in the opening piece, the well-known farce, *A Regular Fix*, and the character of "Hugh de Brass" was one after his own heart, affording him ample opportunity for the display of his lighter talents.

The 5th January, 1892, found him filling the title *rôle* in *Henry VIII.*, a character which had been specially marked out by the profession as one of his most successful renderings. A better Henry than Terriss was not to be desired, so far as all externals went (*see* Frontispiece). But this

observation is not intended to imply that his interpretation of the character was not excellent as
well. Yet it was, of course, the outward resem-
blance and bearing that at first appealed to the
audience, and as represented by him, the King
might have stepped from a canvas by Holbein.
The manner, too, was good ; there was all the proverbial "bluffness," with command as well ; and
as Terriss and Irving took their places, a striking
study was provided of King and Cardinal.

In the production of *Richelieu* on the 7th May,
1892, he appeared as the "Chevalier de Mauprat " ;
and on the 10th November, as "Edgar," in *King
Lear.*

When, on February 6th, 1893, *Becket*, by Alfred,
first Lord Tennyson, was produced, Terriss was
" Henry II.," and in this he met with his accustomed success. It was in this year that the entire
Lyceum company appeared, by command, before
Her Majesty at Windsor Castle. During the
progress of the play the Queen repeatedly led the
applause, and after the drama was over sent for
Henry Irving, Miss Terry, Miss Ward, and

"HENRY II." IN *BECKET*

From a Photo by Window & Grove

Terriss, and congratulated them upon the success to which they had contributed. The Queen furthermore was pleased to express her pleasure at witnessing the play itself.

On one occasion, when a big rehearsal was taking place at the Lyceum, and the air was getting rather blue from the severity of the indefatigable actor-manager, Terriss by his ready wit prevented an explosion. So exactly and conscientiously are the actors trained on the Lyceum stage that, in certain situations, the lessee insists on the various characters keeping the same number of feet apart on each representation. A minor scene was being rehearsed, and one *ingenue*, who, quite unable to remember and keep in her proper position, was on the point of hysterics, was checked in time, by Terriss coming forward and saying in his characteristic way, " Now then, guv'nor, leave it to me "; and he then proceeded to pace out the steps in a mincing way, that was such an outrageous caricature of Sir Henry, that even he laughed more heartily than the others at the libel, and the situation was saved.

At the conclusion of the London season Terriss once more accompanied his chief on an American tour. The company visited most of the more important cities, playing *Much Ado about Nothing*, *Charles I.*, *Becket*, *The Merchant of Venice*, *Nance Oldfield*, *The Bells*, etc., and meeting with an enthusiastic reception wherever they appeared.

Writing during this visit, a member of the company said :—

"We have travelled thousands of miles, from San Francisco to the borders of British Columbia, passing up valleys and round the sides of the Sierra Nevada mountains, enjoying at every turn the most beautiful scenery, the grandeur of which beggars description. I can now see the summit of Mount Shasta, covered with eternal snow, rising 16,000 feet above the level of the sea, the ascension of which, when we arrived at the very high altitude, made the eyes ache and the blood rush to the head.

"Night closes in as our special still speeds along, shutting from view this mighty work of Nature, and we wake the following morning to find ourselves on the shores of the Puget Sound of British Columbia. Thence onward along the course of the mighty Columbia River, upon whose banks are the encampments of the Red Indian and the home of the grisly bear, and here salmon are so plentiful that a twenty-pounder can be bought for sixpence.

"Onward again for three nights and days, through the gray alkali desert, where not a living thing is to be seen—indeed, nothing but man can exist—during which time we have lived in an atmosphere of dust—dust in our food, dust in our drink, dust in our coverlet—dust everywhere. At last we reach the twin cities of St. Paul and Minneapolis, which are situated at the source of the mighty Mississippi, thence onward to the great western metropolis, Chicago, where the rag-tag and bob-tail of humanity of the Western Continent are mingling with the eastern millionaires. Here, amidst murders, assassinations, strikes, and anarchy, we dwell for a month, and once more return to the welcome city of New York, where a hearty greeting awaits us. Here it is that we opened the New Abbey's Theatre with Tennyson's *Becket*. It was certainly a gala night in the annals of theatrical and social circles, the members of the diplomatic corps and men of letters and science honouring the occasion by their presence.

" Miss Millward (who has made such a marked impression as 'Queen Eleanor' in *Becket*) had the honour of speaking the first words in the new house, her first lines being, 'Dost love this Becket, this son of a London merchant?' etc. ; and at the termination of the play there was little doubt that they *did* love it, for of the enthusiastic manner in which the piece was received there was not the slightest doubt, Henry Irving, Miss Terry, Terriss, and Miss Millward receiving call upon call for their admirable impersonations.

"Our stay in New York was made doubly pleasant by the social entertainments which were given everywhere to the leading members of the company; and the beautiful drive along the Hudson River and Central Park, the innumerable trips across the harbour, and the visits to the thousand and one places of interest which

"DON PEDRO" IN *MUCH ADO ABOUT NOTHING*

From a Photo by W. & D. DOWNEY

abound in the neighbourhood were thoroughly enjoyed.

"The hand of the clock was upon midnight, ushering in the New Year, as our special once more was speeding on its way to Boston, and it was with feelings of love and affection, thinking of the old folks in England, that we burst into the refrain, 'Home, Sweet Home,' and many a silent tear was hurriedly wiped away as kindly thoughts and wishes rose in our breasts for those we loved."

Terriss wrote his impressions of America as seen through the actor's spectacles. He said :—

"I consider that Americans are a play-going race, fonder, far fonder, of all that pertains to the drama than we in Great Britain. They are quicker in seeing a point. There is an earnest spontaneity about their applause, and the actor must certainly be troubled with a sluggish liver who is not stirred to something like reciprocity when an American audience 'rises' to the occasion.

"In England—and only those who have passed some years before the footlights can speak with certainty on this matter—it is very difficult to gauge whether you have the true ear of the house.

"Not to put too delicate a point on it, one is not always sure whether one is playing to the gallery, to the stalls, to the pit, or to all three. Divided sympathies are by no means uncommon. I have before now seen Olympus in ecstasies, while the pit has yawned and the stalls frowned ; and again in the same *rôle* I have noted another actor reverse the process, while yet a third has secured the suffrages of the entire 'front.'

" In America this splitting of interests is rarely met with. The Theatre as a whole either madly dotes on you, or coldly and impassively sits you out once.

" Socially the actor in America is received everywhere, though, for the matter of that, the actor in England, so long as he preserves his self-respect, holds pretty much the same position now that education has swept away class prejudices.

" The fair sex in America appear to be dominant in matters theatrical. If the ladies, for example, approve a play or a certain actor, they seem to join hands and support their opinion with such tenacity of purpose that failure is impossible, and a momentary success is guaranteed. The men, too, tacitly accept the position, and seem to take it for granted that the acumen of the feminine brain is, histrionically speaking, superior to their own. They follow dumbly in the wake of the dear creatures, and I am not aware that they could do very much better. Once having gained the right side of the ladies, an actor can leave the rest to Providence and the checktaker.

" In England, I need hardly say this is all reversed ; the *genus homo* is consulted by his wife and daughters as to where to go, and the deference to his judgment where ' mumming ' is concerned is all but universal.

" I found the American race one of the most hospitable and free-hearted folk of the world's teeming millions I have met; and as I have explored a good many corners of our planet, I can conceive of no finer pleasure excursion for an actor—at least a juvenile actor—than a short playing tour from New York to San Francisco.

"The broad burly arms of America's Bohemians are held out, and there are hand-grips and pleasant greetings from jolly good fellows you have never met before. They mean all they say; the large class of Society eagerly welcomes you, and makes much of you, and what is better than all else, you feel that it is not the 'lionizing' sentiment which is actuating your hosts, but the wish to make a fellow feel at home three thousand miles from his own hearth.

"Now a word as to the theatres themselves. These are all round more perfect play-houses, both structurally and acoustically, than our English houses, and the general air of comfort about them is, I take it, one strong reason for the existence of the extensive community of American playgoers.

"We were travelling by special train from New York to San Francisco, and when we arrived at Cheyenne, a station at the foot of the Rocky Mountains, we found that we were twelve hours behind time. Fearing that we should be late for our opening performance, I thought our only

chance was to try an application of the 'Almighty
Dollar.' I did this to the driver in the shape of
a ten-dollar bill, asking at the same time to be
allowed to ride on the engine. The result was
that we ascended and descended the Rockies at a
far greater speed than had ever before been at-
tained, and when it became known that the increased oscillation, as we sped through the rugged
defiles, across the slender bridges that spanned the
yawning ravines, and through the snow sheds, was
due to the erratic driving of a Thespian, prayers
were offered up for the safe arrival of the troupe
at San Francisco. Crossing the suspension bridge
over the Niagara Rapids by night, the mists from
the mighty falls falling like myriads of sparks
from the water as the rays of the white winter
moon played upon it after its leap of 700 ft., and
glittering in every direction, was decidedly a novel
and exhilarating experience. So, too, was sleighing
at lightning speed in ice-boats over the splendid
Lake Ontario, and flying like birds upon the wing
—also in ice-boats—over the frozen surface of the
mighty St. Lawrence River. Toboganning, too,

at the rate of a hundred miles an hour is a luxury one must go to America to fully appreciate. Then, when we were travelling, the temperature was sometimes thirty degrees below zero, and petroleum had to be burned under the engine to prevent the joints from freezing. For more than a week at a stretch we were in the train day and night without even alighting, so that you see even starring in the States has its hardships.

" As we travel through the States the immensity of the country impresses one. In Great Britain the run from Aberdeen to Euston makes one feel that the right little, tight little island is a bit of a misnomer after all, and that the 'little' is an adjective that might with safety be omitted; but in the States the distances are appalling. Of course, one knows the actual linear measurement in miles and furlongs between New York and Chicago; but try the journey, and the feeling of space begins to grow on one until the mind can dwell on little else.

" Every man should love his native land and feel proud of it. The American does this and more;

he revels in the vastness of his country. No one who has traversed it can wonder at the transparent boastfulness which sometimes makes a full-blooded Yankee believe that the world begins at Manhattan and ends at the Port of Monterey.

"The engineering feats appear marvellous. One is absolutely lost in wonderment when contemplating the Brooklyn Bridge, those gigantic structures thrown across the Mississippi at St. Louis, the truly marvellous bridge across Niagara, and the monster hotels everywhere, which surpass the highest caravanserais of fairydom.

"The go-ahead characteristics of the nation speak out in every city, street, and side-walk. Nothing is old—everything fresh and delightful. Can I put the matter more forcibly? Everything they do is great; their chief trait—a trait I admire like all people who possess but little of it—energy."

CHAPTER V

HIS LAST ENGAGEMENTS

A FTER seven pleasant years' association with the Lyceum, Terriss left the company, and for the future made the Adelphi his headquarters. But he was not allowed to leave his old companions without some tokens of the good fellowship which existed between them. The company gave him a very handsome loving cup, while the stage hands presented him with a gold-mounted riding whip.

It was in September, 1894, that he again assumed his favourite character of Adelphi hero, in Messrs. Haddon Chambers and B. C. Stephenson's drama, *The Fatal Card*, and his old admirers found him as much to their liking as ever. His grand acting in the terrible murder

THE GIRL I LEFT BEHIND ME
From a Photo by Window & Grove

"LIEUT. KEPPELL" IN *ONE OF THE BEST*

From a Photo by the Craotint Portrait Co.

■

scene in this play will not readily be forgotten. In *The Girl I Left Behind Me*, the play which followed, he was described as being an object-lesson to melodramatic actors. " How clear and distinct fell every sentence ! How modulated, careful, and unexaggerated was the trained style ! How picturesque was the actor's bearing and every gesture ! There was a grip and command in each sentence. He was vigorous and virile to the backbone."

The next production was the *Swordsman's Daughter*, by Clement Scott and B. C. Stephenson, in December, 1895, and it will be remembered, if for nothing else, as affording Terriss an opportunity for the grandest display of histrionic power he had as yet given. In the third act, in which the father, previously paralyzed, regains strength at the news of his daughter's disgrace, by mere force of will, in order to avenge the dishonour, Terriss rose to the sublime. Following this came *One of the Best*, by George Edwards and Seymour Hicks, and it did not require days, but merely hours, before all London was rushing to see their favourite as the handsome young officer "Lieutenant Dudley Keppell."

The character of the hero is such as must appeal to all. Those who witnessed the performance will never forget the debonair, bright-natured, romantic, loving boy of Terriss in the first two acts of the play, and the crushed man with the bleeding heart, the man grey with grief, yet firm and resolute in his terrible despair, in the third most dramatic scene. It seems, as every honour and medal is stripped and wrenched from him, that it is his very flesh which is being torn and lacerated. Involuntary sobs of stifled anguish rise to the throat at such cruelly degrading treatment of so splendid a soldier ; and then the last superbly triumphant entrance, when the dark clouds of sorrow have been swept away, and there is nothing left but silver—one shining, radiant gleam of silver—for the troubled path is cleared of thorns and pitfalls, and in their place stand roses. It is all very human, and distinctly beautiful in sentiment.

"Terriss was not William Terriss. He was

"LIEUT. DUDLEY KEPPELL" IN *ONE OF THE BEST*

From a Photo by the Craotint Portrait Co.

"LIEUT. DUDLEY KEPPELL" IN *ONE OF THE BEST*

■

young 'Lochinvar'—suddenly and mysteriously he changed himself into a handsome Scottish lad of five-and-twenty. By his presence, by his bearing, by his voice, by his courtesy, and by that one word—so important on the stage—charm—he breathed into this drama that spirit of romance which the crusty, soured pessimists and cynics so much deride."

In 1896, *Boys Together* was put on. The critic of the *Daily Mail*, writing on the first performance, says:—

"Messrs. Haddon Chambers and Comyns Carr have written a play so thrilling and exciting that the tension at times was almost painful. If it be the province of the dramatist to grip an audience in a vice, to make it hold its breath till the curtain falls and the strain is released, and a great shout of pleasure comes from pit and gallery and stalls, then *Boys Together* has proved its authors to be dramatists indeed. To have written a play in which the ability of Mr. William Terriss has such scope as it never had before is a triumph of the writers ; to have grasped to the full the splendid moments that the authors have provided is a triumph for Mr. William Terriss. Never had dramatists finer interpreter—never had actor finer chance. Mr. Terriss's success, the authors' success, came from no subtle introspection, no acute analysis of character, no Meissonier-like minuteness. It came from splendid force, bold colour, an attack that was masterly in its uncompromising directness and strength. *Boys Together* is melodrama naked and unshamed ; as melodrama let it be judged. The new Adelphi play was written to interest and amuse ; it fulfils this, its primary purpose, to the full. But it has another and a more important effect even than this. The great shout that went up when Major Villars—a prisoner in the Soudan —hears of the fall of Khartoum and refuses to believe the news—to believe that England has consented to desert Gordon, the bravest soldier that ever breathed; that, if his country has played so mean a part, English blood and treasure will sooner or later have to be spent to repair the fatal blunder—the great shout that went up was an object-lesson in patriotism. The British public

"GERALD AUSTIN" IN *BOYS TOGETHER*

From a Photo by W. & D. DOWNEY

"GERALD AUSTIN" IN *BOYS TOGETHER*

From a Photo by ALFRED ELLIS

does not forget, and fortune has favoured the Adelphi management; for the desert scene they have given us with such truth and completeness, the period they have revived, the time when Gordon died, is to-day in the minds of us all. Villars is bound, helpless, almost dying, to a rock; then comes one of the great scenes of the drama— Forsyth twits and insults him; Villars prays to be released; Forsyth leaves him to die, but his cords are cut by Maryam, and he swears to her an oath to be avenged. Here it was that Mr. Terriss roused his audience to the supreme pitch of enthusiasm, as well he deserved to do. Passion overcame his weakness; the voice that had been harshed and cracked rang out again; the frame that had been bent by torture was straight once more. No more startling a denunciation has been heard from the stage than that delivered by Mr. William Terriss, ere overcome by his weakness he faints. It may safely be said at this moment the actor touched a higher point than ever before. He carried the house with him; the curtain had to be raised again and again. There were no half lights here—no restrained force.   Mr. Terriss rose to the situation, and carried everything before him."

Black-Ey'd Susan was the next production, a play which in these days has an old-fashioned

A VOICE FROM THE PAST!
Mr. J. P. COOKE "TIP UP YOUR FLIPPER MY LAD — I'M NOT DEAD YET!"

(From the *Illustrated Sporting and Dramatic News*)

aroma, and yet a certain amount of charm for the sea-loving inhabitants of England.

One of the greatest of our nautical writers has said, "To know Jack you must have eaten with him, slept with him, worked with him, and shared in his hardships and in his joys."

"GERALD AUSTIN" IN *BOYS TOGETHER*

From a Photo by the Crantini Portrait Co.

"COMTE DE CANDALE" IN *A MARRIAGE OF CONVENIENCE*

From a Photo by ALFRED ELLIS

HIS LAST ENGAGEMENTS

Many of those who have sat in the comfortable stalls of the Adelphi Theatre and seen Terriss battling with the stormy surf, left alone on rafts, and undergoing the various vicissitudes incidental to descriptive dramatic action, perhaps little knew that he had passed through all these things in real life. He could play the sailor to the life.

Perhaps no other actor known to this generation could have brought back to the Adelphi such an antiquated example of theatrical production as *Black-Ey'd Susan*, yet Terriss' breezy air, his rough-and-ready method, his ability to sing a nautical ditty and to dance a hornpipe, and his command of feeling, secured for the piece a long run. On its withdrawal an American company took possession of the theatre, and Terriss being at liberty appeared at the Haymarket, in the adaptation *A Marriage of Convenience*. In this, as the "Comte de Candale," he showed he had lost none of his gift of comedy, and after his long course of melodrama it came as a relief to him to appear once more in a part belonging to his former line. The younger generation knew him only as a melodramatic hero, and he was pleased to have the opportunity of showing some of his other talents. But his contract with the Messrs. Gatti entailed his return to the Adelphi, and *In the Days of the Duke*, by Haddon Chambers and Comyns Carr, showed him as an elderly man in the prologue, and his assumption of age won him a large amount of commendation. This was his last original part. When the piece failed to draw, a revival of the American play *Secret Service* took place, and in this, as "Captain Thorne," he made his last appearance. He had to follow the successful feature in the original production of the play, the author and actor, Mr. Gillett, who is a master in the arts of pantomime and expression. He acquitted himself admirably. "He could not, and he would not, forget the English style that has endeared him to the public," says the *Daily Telegraph*. "He was strong, powerful, virile, dogged, and determined as ever; but he scouted the idea that 'Captain Thorne,' plucky devil as he was, had nerves. Never on his English face—it cannot be anything else—was the worn,

IN THE DAYS OF THE DUKE

From a Photo by ALFRED ELLIS

harassed, nervous expression of a man who turns spy for the love of country. William Terriss is so frank that he cannot suggest intrigue in any form or shape. His 'Captain Thorne' is a downright, determined, devil-may-care fellow, as strong as a lion, but with no suspicion of the snake about him. Yet 'Captain Thorne' must be in some remote way connected with a snake, for is he not a spy? But these delicacies of criticism did not affect an Adelphi audience in the least. They had got their Terriss, and he loved an honest girl, and he was shot in the hand by a rival, and like Jim Bludso, he did his duty and 'went for it thar and then,' and that was quite enough for the pit."

It was during the run of this piece that his career was so suddenly, so tragically ended, and in the waves of regret, horror, and sorrow that swept over England, aye, and America as well, on receipt of the sad news, none was more sincere and more heartfelt than that originating in the hearts of his old friends the Adelphi audiences. By them he was simply adored; he was their hero, no matter what character he was playing, and for him they chiefly looked, no matter what the play might be. In stalls and boxes, pit and gallery, it was the same thing; they one and all pinned their faith on Terriss, and Terriss did not disappoint them. He had been the recipient of rings sent round by infatuated ladies, and bunches of flowers had been thrust into his hand on his way to the stage-door by servant-girls, with timid requests that he would accept them. Nor was the devotion to be wondered at.

He was cheery, he was electric, he was sympathetic; when he came upon the scene he brightened everything. If the audience had lapsed into lethargy, he was the one to arouse it, and to stir his colleagues to impulse. He felt what he did, and meant what he said. He was held in good faith by the public; he never took a liberty with them, and never let his interest flag —the last night as well as the first, to good houses or to bad, he never lost the grip of his part.

He might have played one character better than another, but he was never known to scamp his work, or to fail to give any part in which he appeared nerve, muscle, and fibre.

He never seemed destined to bid farewell to youth in any character he impersonated. He was the embodiment of health, life, sparkle, and manly vigour.

To the public he was an ideal. Somehow he had the knack of bringing into the atmosphere of our daily and sometimes disheartening life a vitality and a fascination that were absolutely infectious.

Terriss was a host in himself. He was one of our most typical English actors, and the familiar adjective of "Breezy" bestowed upon him was characteristic of the man and the artist. Such a temperament as this, buoyant and optimistic, was of great value to a popular theatre. He was an actor incapable of pulling a long face.

An audience was instinctively the better for an Adelphi play with a deep draught of Terriss thrown in.

CHAPTER VI

HOME LIFE AND CHARACTER

TERRISS would often tell his friends that he found the chief source of enjoyment in his tranquil home life. "The Cottage" in Bedford Park savours of rusticity and repose. It is a little building, with red gabled roof and latticed windows, situated "far from the madding crowd."

The interior is a perfect picture gallery. Close to the porch door hangs a portrait of the host as "Squire Thornhill," flanked by photographs of Mr. Henry Pettitt and Messrs. Agostino and Stefano Gatti. The stained glass barely allows you to decipher the inscription, "To dear Terriss, in kind remembrance of old times, Sincerely yours, Henry Irving," on an engraving of Hamlet, which seems to guard the staircase; and in two groups hard by you recognise "Dear Terriss" again, not in

154

"THE COTTAGE," BEDFORD PARK

any famous character, as you might reasonably suppose, but firstly in his shirt-sleeves as an active member of the West London Quoit Club, and secondly with his friends the late Sir Augustus Harris and James Fernandez, as the life and soul of an autumn outing of the Drury Lane Fund to Burnham Beeches.

When you paid him a visit, and your name was announced, there was no waiting to be ushered into his study, but he came out to greet you himself, and would hail you and welcome you to Bedford Park in that melodious voice which has given pleasure to thousands.

He would carry you off with him for a tour round the back garden, where you would meet with a series of surprises.

When Terriss first located himself at " The Cottage " he planted an apple tree, in which he manifested the greatest interest. It blossomed in profusion, and he predicted that it would be a prolific tree. But a bitter frost played such havoc with those blossoms that, to a great extent, his interest relaxed for a time, but was restored on his finding a sample of fruit thereon. This, the only apple, ripened, and was at length placed on the table; and those who partook of it (he shared it out equally) were more than once reminded by Terriss that "I grew this in my own garden, and don't you forget it."

A visit to his cherished aviary of singing birds might probably follow; thence your steps would be directed to the cosy drawing-room, and on the Chinese cabinet being opened, he would show you his medals, faded portraits of himself as a Blue Coat boy, midshipman, etc., and miniatures taken in early days. He would ask you to go over his picture gallery, containing portraits of Clement Scott, G. R. Sims, and a host of friends unknown to the stage and literature. You would admire his paintings by some old masters, and he would not forget to point out the Loving Cup, which occupies a prominent place on the mantelpiece. Passing from this apartment he would manifest considerable pride as he referred you to his family group and ancestors which hang in the hall.

HOME LIFE AND CHARACTER

Ascending the Queen Anne staircase, he would take you to his tiny study and hand you the cigar-box. Here you were prepared for a stroll round Bedford Park. To the inhabitants of this residential suburb he was a familiar figure. Terriss on the stage was most elegant in dress, but off it a thorough Bohemian in attire. As often as not he wore a tweed suit with a soft-crowned hat resting lightly on his head ; and not one in a hundred of his admirers would have recognised in him the spruce and dainty-looking hero of the Adelphi.

In half an hour or so you were seated in the snuggest of parlours. Here he kept his books and papers. Terriss had many irons in the fire, and up to a certain point was a remarkably shrewd business man ; but by some he was considered too cautious in his dealings to be a really successful financier. He took care always to be on the safe side. You could seldom get him to talk "shop." If you happened to catch him in the right humour, he would tell you that he took an eminently business-like view of his profession, and that he would do his best to amuse in the capacity of a clown, if fate were to cast him for such a part.

He owed everything to his own perseverance and hard work. He had no favours shown him, and no one to help him to achieve popularity. His motto was " *Carpe diem.*"

Speaking of the art, he declared that his sympathies were entirely with the late Sir Augustus Harris, and that he thoroughly believed in the motto, " A fair field and no favour." Art as a means to the end was all very well. It was useful, like the fourth wheel of a coach, but it would not of itself drive the coach. Give him a theatre worked on a sound commercial basis, interspersed with art occasionally if you liked— as a dressing he believed it to be useful.

He also held that there was as much art in portraying the feelings in melodrama as in the most classical drama. He considered *Harbour Lights* as important a play and as difficult to act as many others deemed more classic.

At the same time he was a great lover of his

MRS. TERRISS

profession, although he was constantly speaking against it. He had a kind, soft, generous heart, even if he sometimes put on a hard, selfish appearance. His great horror was to be thought sentimental. After his death, among the many hundreds of letters of sympathy and regret which were received by his family was one from an unknown woman, telling how he had met her one night, and by his kindly aid and advice she had been saved from premeditated suicide, and was then earning her living in a respectable manner.

A needy actor, with a parcel, under his arm to whom Terriss had often shown acts of friendship, cannoned against him one day in the Strand.

" Hullo, dear boy, what the devil are you doing now ? " asked Terriss.

" I've done with the stage and am travelling in wall papers."

" Why, are you still out of an engagement ? " asked Terriss. " Come to my office, and I'll give you a note to take round to M——," naming a well-known actor-manager.

A note was written, and the other prepared to take it.

Terriss glanced at his appearance, which, to put it mildly, lacked an air of prosperity. Taking off his gold watch and chain, and detaching the button-hole from his coat,—

" Put these on ; they'll smarten you up a bit," he said.

And as the impecunious one was going out of the door, Terriss added,—

" Here, you can't go round with the parcel of wall papers. Leave them with me. I'll look after them. Perhaps I'll book you some orders."

The applicant was successful in obtaining the desired engagement, and having returned and thanked Terriss for his kindness, the elated man was about to leave the dressing-room, when Terriss yelled out,—

"Hi, you're not going to purloin my personal property ! Give me back the watch and chain, and the button-hole."

The watch and chain were at once returned, but the possessor was reluctant to part with the button-hole, and asked if he might keep it. Terriss turned to his *confrères* who were with him, and remarked, good-naturedly,—

"I got the man an engagement, became a commercial traveller in the wall-paper line on his behalf, lent him my personal property, and now the bounder wants to sneak my button-hole." But he gave it him all the same; and the man still has it in his possession.

He was very unostentatious in his generosity, and above all things endeavoured to spare a poorer man's feelings. He often had friends, not so well off as himself, playing cards with him at Bedford Park, and though he would adapt the stakes to their means, still if he thought they had lost more than was convenient to them, he would quietly put half a sovereign or so under their plates when they afterwards sat down to supper. And in the case of others, who perhaps had some way to go home, he would slip some silver into the pockets of their overcoats, "just to pay for the cab," so that they might find it afterwards, and not know where it had come from.

He was a most methodical man, and at home would have everything in its proper place. He considered confusion a heinous sin, and would treat the party guilty of it accordingly.

A true Bohemian, he found the usages of the most polite society just a little irksome.

He revelled in chess and cards, and excelled in both, while in later years he took up cycling as an outside pastime. In his youth he was a "sprinter" of very high calibre, and few men could beat him at a hundred yards. His fame as a swimmer is pretty generally known, but the following cutting from a local paper may not be without interest:—

"A swimming handicap, which created considerable interest, took place on Thursday, September 9th, 1869, at the Marylebone Baths, the prize being a handsome silver cup, which, after a spirited contest, was won by Mr. William Terriss. Since the race the gentlemen frequenters of these baths have formed themselves into a club, to be called ' The Leander,' and which already numbers sixty members." Terriss was their first captain.

He all along sought to drill into the minds

of his sons the paramount importance of their becoming good swimmers, and whether they agreed
with him or not on the point, he persisted in having
his way. When the boys were quite young, he
took them for a row, ostensibly with the object of
giving them a treat. Having got well out to sea,
he insisted upon their "dipping." With reluctance
they agreed, but very shortly found themselves in
a terrible plight. Terriss was in his element, and
embraced the opportunity of showing his offsprings
the tactics to be observed under the circumstances
in which they were then placed. He was, however, hardly allowed time to go through the lesson,
before he was called upon to rescue the pair, who
had from fear or fatigue released their hold of
the sides of the boat. It was not until positively
obliged to do so that he would allow them to
resume their places in the boat, and make tracks
homeward bound. He taught his daughter in the
same way, but he secured the young lady by a
rope.

One day in August, 1885, off the South Fore-
land, three lads were bathing, one of whom got

out too far, and was seized with cramp before he could reach the shore. He cried out for assistance, which his two companions were not able to render. It so happened that Terriss and his son Tom were yachting in the vicinity, and Terriss, seeing the poor fellow in distress, lowered the lugsail, and without divesting himself of clothing, jumped overboard. He seized the lad just in the nick of time. A gallant rescue of two children from drowning by Terriss was also reported from Barnes. It appears that a child fell into the river, and a lad jumped in to endeavour to save it. Both were sinking, when Terriss swam to them and got them out. He was the recipient of two medals from the Royal Humane Society.

In connection with his aquatic performances, it may not be out of place to recall one of his many jokes. He and a brother, who was also an expert swimmer, were spending the week-end at one of our favourite watering-places on the South Coast, and while on the pier Terriss induced his relative to do a little gymnastic exercise on the rail, with the result that the gentleman, somehow or other, fell

TERRISS'S YOUNGEST SON

overboard. Terriss appeared greatly distressed, and called loudly for help. Naturally a large crowd soon gathered round the spot, and numbers of people were exceedingly active in lowering life-buoys to the man in peril below. "I will save my friend, if I die in the attempt," cried Terriss, at the same time divesting himself of his coat, and plunging in. He soon reached his brother, bringing him ashore in triumph. The Humane Society, it is said, heard of what they considered an act of bravery, and would have made their usual presentation had not Terriss disclosed the premeditated joke.

Terriss was justly proud of his clear-cut face, and also of his slim, manly figure. A few days before his death he told Dr. Edmund Owen that he had recently received a violent shock. As he was coming up Regent Street in the bright light of a morning sun, two ladies passed in front of him, and one of them said, loud enough for him to hear, "That's Terriss! Goodness me! How old he looks!"

For racing he did not seem to have the least

taste, and when any one asked him what horse he was going to back, he would say, "I'm going to back a little filly I've often backed before; I've never won anything on it, yet, strange to say, I've never lost a penny." "Oh, whatever horse is that?" might have been the inquiry. "A little filly called Common Sense, ridden by Tommy Let-it-alone," was the invariable answer.

He was exceedingly slow in studying a part, and always did the work in bed, late at night, or early in the morning.

Another peculiarity of his was that he would never have a play read to him, but on a MS. being submitted, he would carefully go through it, and write his opinion on the outside. One of the last letters, if not *the* last, he ever wrote, was to an old friend in connection with this very subject.

"ADELPHI THEATRE,

"*Dec.* 15, 1897.

" My dear Hunt,—

"Glad to hear from you. I would not have a MS. read to me if there were millions in it.

Send it on, and I will run through it. Wishing
you every success. With love.

"Your old friend,

"WILL TERRISS."

Of course round such a popular actor as Terriss
many a story and romance grew up. For instance,
it was said he had been in the Royal Navy, had
been shipwrecked, had been at Oxford, had been
a doctor, and many other fictions, and it was his
pleasure to foster them, rather than deny them,
until he grew almost to believe them true himself, and many a good story he told, fitting the
cap to himself, whose origin, had it been sifted
out, would have been found to be rather more in
fiction than fact. But of the romances woven
around his name by others than himself, the following, overheard one evening in the Adelphi, is
a fair sample. The narrator was a lady, who,
hearing her neighbours speak of Terriss, inter-
posed with : " Yes, is he not splendid ? So good
looking ; but such a sad life, my dears, such a
sad life is his. Some years ago, when he was

quite young, he was in Paris, gazing at the Venus of Milo, when a young girl came up and also gazed at the same object. Terriss turned, and then started, and looked earnestly at her, for she was the most beautiful being he had ever seen—well, it was the old, old story. He managed to get an introduction, and before a fortnight had passed they were engaged. Soon he had to go back to London to fulfil his engagement; she stayed behind to study art under one of the great French masters. Six months elapsed, and Terriss received a note from her, breaking off the engagement, but giving no sufficient reason. He hurried off to Paris, but could find no trace of her or her guardian. He never saw her again, for within a year she died, sending him a letter explaining all. She was the daughter of some great criminal, and had never known this until the day she wrote to him, saying she loved him too well to bring him dishonour. Terriss has never married; he will never speak to a woman if he can help it; and he never acts upon the day she died."

"Thoroughness was the dominant quality in the nature of William Terriss," writes a very old friend of his, "in his business relations, artistic connections, friendships and affections—that one word covered all—thoroughness."

If he had not genius in the sense we understand it, he had the capacity for taking infinite pains, and he was ever ready to listen to suggestions, and try his best to carry out the ideas of others. He did not, as many actors do with small ability and self-confidence, "pooh-pooh" an author or manager's wishes; and I well remember the late Mr. W. G. Wills, saying to me of Terriss after a rehearsal of *Olivia* at the Court Theatre: "He will do; he listens to suggestions, and tries to work out what we want."

Now and then Terriss put his spoke into the wheel of an academic controversy, and mostly a good sound workmanlike spoke it was. When the conduct of the demonstrative "first-nighters" was the subject of discussion in the *Era*, Terriss ranged himself on the side of the "first-nighter," declaring frankly that he liked to be applauded, but

also he admitted the right of the "first-nighter"
to hiss. "It's all very well," he said, "to claim
the indulgence due to ladies and gentlemen, but
artists should remember that they are actors or
actresses when they are on the boards ; and if
they wish to be treated as ladies and gentlemen
only, they had better remain in that privacy with
which the public have no right to interfere, and
where they will be alike free from public applause
and public censure." A sentiment which Mr.
Punch labelled "Number One Adelphi Terriss."
And he hit the right nail on the head in a letter
of his to the *Daily Telegraph* on the Shakespeare-
Bacon controversy, in which the lines of Terriss's
argument might have had for their text the words
which Thomas à Kempis wrote long ago : "Search
not who spoke this or that, but mark what is
spoken." Terriss argued sensibly and bluntly to
this effect, that it did not matter a sou who
wrote the marvellous collection of plays which
have been handed down to us through such a
length of time as the works of William Shakespeare ; and that if it could be proved to-morrow,

beyond the slightest possibility of doubt, that they were written by Bacon or Burleigh or Queen Elizabeth, we should not be really one jot the happier or the wiser. We have got the plays ; they were our precious, imperishable possession. Why should we care two straws as to the precise nomenclature of the dead-and-gone man of genius who penned them? As well waste our time in bewailing the MSS. from Shakespeare's hands that may have perished in the flames through the carelessness of a general servant ; as well hunt after the authorship of the Book of Job, or weary our spirits in seeking to identify Koheleth.

CHAPTER VII

HIS DEATH AND BURIAL

TERRISS had laid down his plans for the future. He contemplated a twelve weeks' tour of the suburban and provincial theatres, to be followed by a tour through South Africa and Australia.

He often said that after this was accomplished he would retire from the stage. He had made the proverbial golden egg, and it was his desire to enjoy the rest of his life in country surroundings.

He did not believe in lasting glory, but rather that, whatever a reputation an actor might make, and to what summit he might rise, both he and his work would soon be forgotten.

An actor's popularity being of such an ephemeral nature, so short lived, he held it better to bid adieu

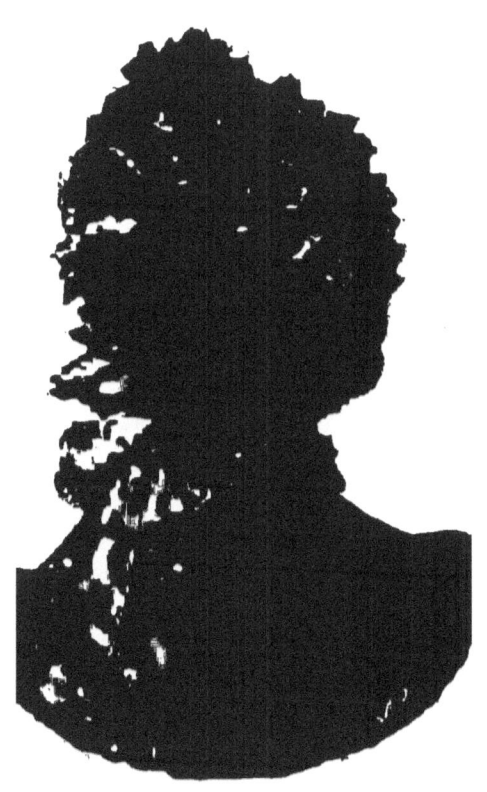

THE LATE MRS. G. H. LEWIN
(TERRISS'S MOTHER)

to a generous play-going public whilst still fresh and
in favour, instead of lagging on until he became a
decrepit old gentleman.

On the other hand he considered that the results
of the work of a great actor, like Henry Irving for
instance, would always be felt, but such as his own
could not possibly leave behind a mark for good or
evil.

He was not, however, permitted to carry out his
plan, for his career of adventure and honest good
work closed with awful suddenness on the evening
of the 16th of December, 1897. He and a friend
were about to enter the private door of the Adelphi
Theatre, where he was playing in *Secret Service*,
when a maniac's stab put an end to this gay, this
generous, this admirable life.

Nature in mournful unison with man responded
to the keynote of sadness struck in countless hearts
by the last solemn rites accompanying the inter-
ment, which took place a few days afterwards
at Brompton Cemetery, where so many of our
popular heroes and heroines of the stage sleep in
peace.

THE LIFE OF WILLIAM TERRISS

It may be said with truth that the funeral was the occasion of one of the greatest public demonstrations of sympathy and respect that London has ever seen.

Not only the heads of the dramatic profession, in which he was so universally loved,—not only the representatives of literature and journalism, but members of every art and craft passed through those mournful gates to pay a last tribute of respect and veneration at the grave of one who, if not a comrade, was at least a friend.

Her Majesty the Queen expressed her sympathy in an eloquent autograph letter addressed to the family as follows :—

" The Queen sends her condolence and deep sympathy to Mrs. William Terriss and family in their sad bereavement. She deeply feels the loss which has robbed the English stage of one of its brightest ornaments."

His Royal Highness the Prince of Wales contributed a wreath, while other floral tributes numbered over one thousand, the forms and colours of which were as striking as their number and beauty.

THE LATE GEORGE HERBERT LEWIN, BARRISTER-AT-LAW

(TERRISS'S FATHER)

There were a ship, and a steering wheel, a globe resting on a Union Jack, and bearing the words, " All the world's a stage," a ladder typical of fame, shields, harps, lyres, cushions, anchors, broken pillars, and innumerable crosses.

The coffin bore the simple inscription :—

WILLIAM CHARLES JAMES LEWIN,

Died 16th December, 1897,

Aged 49 *years.*

When the last solemn words of the ritual had been spoken, the chaplain delivered a brief but eloquent address in praise of the departed actor, and of the profession of which he had been so worthy an ornament. Coming through the streets, the speaker said, he had passed through the ranks of a great crowd animated with a single thought— one of deep respect for the dead, and affectionate sympathy with the friends of him who had gone. It would afford consolation to those whom William Terriss held dear to realize the heartfelt sorrow with which all London—the whole country—regarded their loss. Those who were the late actor's comrades in art—those who worked with him in "the same great profession "—knew all and more than he could tell them of the dead man. If they were doing their duty in that noble calling, they would feel that their reward was always to be found in the appreciation of the public. They must needs derive great satisfaction from the approval of those who called them to the portrayal of the complexities of human life. Their dead friend they were now leaving in the hands of the Almighty, and that was the only keeping to which those who were left behind would entrust him.

Words like these, spoken with deep feeling and conviction, drew their inevitable tribute of tears. It was with moist and trembling eyelids that women and men alike turned from the grave where they had laid their departed brother. Sorrow sat upon each brow as the great congregation slowly dispersed and left the dead actor to his long rest.

A beautiful and impressive memorial service was held at the Chapel Royal, Savoy, at which the same clergyman spoke the following appreciation :—

From a Photo by ALFRED ELLIS

HIS DEATH AND BURIAL

"Which of us who are gathered together could by any possibility have dreamt that such a call would have summoned us here? It is all so sudden and so cruel. One of us, in the very midst of life, health, usefulness, and the esteem of those around him, has been struck down by this cowardly hand. The horror of it flashed through London from east to west, and linked east and west in one common sorrow. The very irony of such a thing appalled us. I think, among all the great testimony which has been pouring out in his memory and honour, there are two passages you must have seen—one, 'I did not know that he had an enemy in life,' and the other, 'I would have risked twenty lives to have saved him.' These sayings are typical of those who knew and loved him best. The manner of it, too, it seems as if we cannot get it out of our minds. The word assassination is, thank God, almost unknown in this England of ours. May it ever remain so. But it is not that of which you would have me to speak in addressing a few words to you this morning. It is rather of himself. A generous, kindly soul has gone. No

longer shall we have those splendid, manly representations of life as it is, as it may be, as
imagination may picture it before us. There is
something that has always very much interested
us in his work. We all at heart have a great
regard for that old Adelphi and the pieces we have
had there for years past, since the time when we
became playgoers, and we know how careful and
good all his efforts were in his own great profession.
But outside that, it is always said of you members
of the dramatic profession that you are a warm-
hearted, enthusiastic, and generous people. From
my own experience I can testify how true it is. I
know what you do when some of you go down in
the battle of life. I know what ready help you
give, and know that at the moment of your success
you think of the dark days which life may have
in store. I know your estimate of each other; it
is as generous as it possibly can be. I know that
the brotherhood and sisterhood which exist
between you are of the closest and kindliest; and
it must be a delight to you to see the outside
public recognising all this in connection with one

of the well-known and leading members of your body. It must be a delight to you that the gifts which he possessed carry with them their impression on the public mind, and raise the whole status and dignity of the actor's profession. He is not dead. He doth not sleep. He has awakened from the dream of life. I grant you that, as men and women, and as Christians, it needs all the power that is within us to rise to the full measure of our faith at such a moment. It is very hard to say, 'It is well.' We can only do it in the sense that we leave our dead friend in the hands of the Great Father who loves and pities each one of us, the God who measures the value of each life as no man or woman among us can ever measure our acts, wishes, deeds, and intentions. And I think that from this gathering, to which you have come with hearts full of sorrow and sympathy, you will go away strengthened. It seems to me only the other day we sat here together, and that I was privileged to address a few words to you on the death of poor Charles Riley. Even if I repeat what I said then, I say you must go back strengthened after such a gathering as this, feeling that your art has such a power in it, that in the steady adherence to duty and the best interpretation of those wonderful dramas and scenes which are in the hands of modern players, you have a great trust, and that if you carry out that trust as a real thing you have a most generous public to witness your work. You will then ever have most appreciative audiences, because they know that there is the best teaching to be found in those scenes of human life which you portray. You feel, not only that sympathy and interest, but the obligation you have to the public. That public is ever ready enough to give you back generously— to give you back your measure running over. Go back to your life, strengthened in the sense that this dead man's kindly life has made a deep impression, not only upon all of you who have been his partners in the work, but has sunk deeply into the hearts of our English people."

CHAPTER VIII

BREEZY BILL

TO his fellow-actors and companions the above was one of the familiar names by which he was known, and he appeared to do his best to deserve it; but there were a few, a very few, to whom he displayed the other side of his character, a side the world at large knew nothing of. He was not always the merry, jovial, restless spirit people imagined him; there were times when he allowed the inner side of his character to be seen, when he gave way to strong emotion, and when he suffered his deeper nature to come to the surface. But these occasions were rare. He thought, and he felt deeply, but those thoughts and feelings he kept, for the most part, to himself. It seemed almost as if he were anxious that the world should know him only in his lighter moods, and as if his somewhat mournful and sombre moments were intended for himself alone. His daughter's very serious illness, and the death of her baby, affected him deeply; and as the little coffin was being lowered into the vault where his mother and he himself now rest, he said to his brother, "Ah, Bob, I feel it won't be long before I shall join her" (meaning his mother).

The Sunday before his death, while at dinner with his family, he told them of a man who had died suddenly of heart disease. By the dramatic way in which he acted the last motion of the man he frightened his wife, and more so when he added, with much emphasis—"A splendid death to die; no lingering illness, no bedside agonies, no doctors, no cries, moans, or tears, heartrending to all; but peace, perfect peace."

Death was a subject on which he would frequently converse; he had no horror nor fear of it, though he seemed to be shadowed by presentiment, and was a thorough believer in predestination. In connection with this his old friend Mr. B. Fargeon writes: "I never heard him utter an

From a Photo by WINDOW & GROVE

unamiable word, and it often struck me that in his views of life and death, which I may mention was a theme upon which he constantly spoke, there was a greater depth than he was generally credited with." Some few weeks before his death, Mrs. Terriss was reading the notices of *Charlotte Corday* in the *Daily Telegraph*, and she happened to say she thought the part of "Marat" would suit him excellently.

He shuddered at the idea, and said: "Ah, no! horrible! I could not bear that scene with the knife; to be stabbed like that seems terrible. I should not like to take that part."

And this sober side was not merely the outcome of mature years; even in the careless days of his youth it was present, if not often visible. One of his very old friends supplies two incidents that well illustrate this. He says :—

" My very first recollection of him (Terriss, dating about 1865) gives me the picture of a handsome and decided young man stepping between and separating two working-men engaged in fistic encounter. There must have been some magnetism about him, for a moment after he laid his hands upon their shoulders and said a few quiet words to them, one combatant silently departed in one direction and the other by another route.

"Another incident I well remember. It occurred in 1869; I think it was 1869. A pair-oared race, a friendly contest, had been arranged between two crews. Dr. Friend Lewin (Terriss' brother), a very powerful oar, and Mr. William Dawson, one of Terriss' oldest and most valued friends, manned one of the boats, whilst poor Terriss (stroke) and myself (bow) were their opponents.

"In preparation for this race we were accustomed to take a daily pull over the course. One morning, a bright morning in early summer, we landed for a few minutes, leaving our boat beside a landing-stage. When we had returned, and were re-seated with the small boy who steered us, trimly prepared for his responsibilities, the young man who looked after the boats gave us a push off. Such a push off that it nearly upset the boat. Terriss turned to me and said, ' Pull in, old man.'

" This done, he stepped from the boat, and, seizing the man by the collar, exclaimed :—

" ' You scoundrel! because you were not satisfied with the money I gave you, you tried to upset our boat. That would not have hurt my friend or myself, but it might have drowned that little boy.'

" The man turned deathly pale, whilst the expression of his countenance and faltering attempt at a denial of the charge left little room for doubt that his guilty intention had been seen through, though for charity's sake I cannot bring myself to believe that he contemplated a fatal catastrophe to crown his malignancy.

" With a superb movement of disdain, and a gesture full of expression, Terriss released his hold of the churl with the words :—

" ' I spare you this time. Live—and learn to be a man.'

" As I recall this incident, I cannot resist the reflection that Terriss' success upon the stage was in considerable measure due to the fact that he had not in heroic situations to 'assume a virtue.' What has been termed 'sublimated' intonation and gesture was really natural to the man himself.

"In no scene subsequently played by him on the boards was there finer treatment of a situation shown than on that summer's morning when, long before the day of his theatrical successes, his own individuality, then histrionically untrained, gave so effective an object-lesson in those indispensable symbols of the greatest histrions, viz., facial expression, voice, and gesture."

But it was in the brighter side of his character that Terriss was best known to his friends and acquaintances. Above all he was a terrible practical joker; even his intimates and relations never felt safe. His own brother said: "I never knew what he would be up to next; he was certain to have you before long." And the more completely he *did* have you, the greater was his delight. Dr. George Field thus relates one of his early freaks :—

"When we were one day walking out together he remarked, 'You see that nice old lady with the

white curls coming along. I am going to kiss her.'
And without more ado, he went up to the old
dame and kissed her. To the naturally indignant
exclamation, 'How dare you, sir!' Terriss, not
a whit abashed, and with the self-command of a
perfect actor, replied,—

" 'Your name, I think, is Jones.'

" ' Nothing of the sort,' she cried ; 'my name
is Smith.' I forget now whether this was her
exact cognomen.

" 'Oh,' said he, 'I have made a most unfortunate
mistake. I quite thought you were my grand-
mother ; you are the very image of her.'

" Whereupon he took off his hat, and was so
profuse in his apologies that, before he left her,
the old lady beamed with smiles, and appeared
quite enchanted with his politeness."

His brother Bob (Friend) was the constant
victim of his jokes, and the following are only
a few samples out of a large stock :—

" I and Will had one day occasion to go up to
the Agricultural Hall at Islington, and we travelled
by 'bus. The interior was pretty full, but there was

one seat at the far end which I took possession of, while Will seated himself close to the door. Away we rumbled, and whether it was that I was tired, or that the 'bus was close, I don't know, but I felt very drowsy, and commenced nodding. I ought to mention that I was anything but smartly dressed that day, having on a rough suit of tweed, and wearing a cap. I had not been taking my ease very long before I heard the words, 'My Lord!' uttered in well-known tones. A cold shiver ran down my back at the sound. Heaven only knew what was coming next, and I felt my one course was to feign sleep. But it was no good; I might have saved myself the trouble. Again the words were repeated, this time somewhat louder, 'My Lord!' and on my refusing to take any notice, I heard the request: 'Might I trouble you, sir, just to touch that gentleman in the corner.' There was no help for it now; I *had* to wake, which I did in as natural a manner as I could assume, with the query, 'Eh, well; what is it? Eh?' 'I merely wished to inquire, my Lord, whether it was at *The Angel* public house you wished to get out?' replied Will, with the

AT 30

From a Photo by W. & D. DOWNEY

utmost gravity. Imagine my feelings, dressed as I then was!

"On another occasion my brother and I were travelling in a third-class smoking carriage from Woolwich to Charing Cross. The compartment was quite full of workmen. Will was sitting opposite me, and apparently in the best of health, when I suddenly saw his eyes close, and his mouth begin to twitch. I was horrified, for I knew only too well what was coming; but I pretended not to notice anything, and gazed out of the window. But almost immediately I received a nudge in the side, and my next-door neighbour said, 'I say, your mate's took bad, I think.' I was forced to look then. 'Oh, it's nothing,' I replied; 'it will soon pass off; leave him alone.' Will probably heard this, for the facial contortions were redoubled, and the other occupants of the carriage were seriously alarmed. 'Here, I say,' exclaimed one, 'you must do something for him; he's dying.' I attempted to make light of it, but general opinion was against me, and I was compelled, while leaning over and shaking him, to whisper : 'For heaven's sake,

Will, come to again ; it's getting beyond a joke.'
And my brother acceded to my request, and in the
most natural manner recovered his senses. I was
congratulating myself on having thus got out of an
unpleasant predicament, for the workmen, misjudg-
ing my indifference, had summed me up as an
unfeeling brute, and were inclined to be nasty, when
to my horror I saw Will feigning a second and
a far more violent fit. It was one of the
truest pieces of imitation I have ever witnessed.
I had to become a most unwilling actor myself
now, in order to restore him to consciousness, and
the end of it was that, instead of continuing our
journey to Charing Cross, our fellow-travellers
compelled me to take my brother out at Cannon
Street, in order to convey him as quickly as possible
to the nearest hospital.

" Another time I was travelling with him on the
Underground, our only companion being an old
gentleman busily engaged with his paper opposite
us. We hadn't proceeded very far, when Will,
with a glance at our companion, leant towards me
and said in a loud stage whisper, ' It's Snodgrass.'

BREEZY BILL

'Oh no, it isn't,' I replied, nervous as to what was coming. 'Oh yes, it is; I'm sure of it. It *must* be'; and then, as I endeavoured to stop him, he bent forward towards the gentleman and said: 'Pardon me, sir, but your name's Snodgrass, I think?' 'No,' said the old gentleman; 'you've made a mistake; it's So-and-so.' 'Not Snodgrass! Really. Well, I never saw so remarkable a likeness. He was an old schoolfellow of ours. I could have sworn you were he. It is curious; you must allow me to shake hands with you.' This the gentleman did. 'Now, Bob, you must shake hands with him too; isn't it a remarkable likeness?' And I had to go through the farce of shaking hands with a perfect stranger I had never seen in my life before. And when we arrived at our station, Will would not leave the carriage before we both had once more gone through the performance, on the strength of an imaginary likeness to a visionary schoolfellow named Snodgrass of all names. Whether the old gentleman saw through him, I am not in a position to say; but I know I felt very thankful when I had left the carriage.

"I and my brother together visited the Paris Exhibition, and the fancy took him to parade the building in a bath chair, and occasionally give a life-like representation of a severe epileptic fit."

Railway carriages appear to have been favourite arenas with Terriss for the display of his powers.

When the new indicator was first placed in the trains on the District Railway system, he regarded it as a novelty, but complained of the name of the advertising firm being placed in bolder type than that of the next station. On one occasion he travelled in a third-class smoking carriage, and disguised himself as a Frenchman. The carriage was well filled with members of the artisan class, who were somewhat amused, if not concerned, at the utterances of the Frenchman. Terriss, who was with one of his sons at the time, spoke in broken English, rolled his eyes, and asked whether the next station was " Mellin's Food, or Keatings." The fellow-passengers appeared to think he was a madman. His son pacified them by saying he was in charge of the lunatic, and he was harmless. Presently, on arriving at his destination,

Terriss threw off his disguise. The workmen appreciated the joke, and Terriss handed them each the price of a refresher.

This was not the only occasion on which he personated an insane person, for once, whilst staying at Roehampton, having heard that a lunatic had escaped, he ascertained what he was like and did his best to represent him. Admirably disguised, he ran past the police station, and the officers noticing him, and believing him to be the lunatic, chased him a great distance. Getting well ahead of them, he seized the opportunity for quickly getting rid of his disguise, and walked back in the direction they were coming. Meeting them, he stopped them and explained matters ; and it would not have been Terriss if his victims did not part with him agreeably satisfied.

Another of his jokes, which, alas ! has lately, in part, been painfully realized, is told by Mrs. Terriss. She and the family were visiting Madame Tussaud's, when her husband, noticing an empty stand covered with the usual red baize, immediately took up his position upon it. He struck an attitude, and remained still and apparently life-less. Presently visitors came that way, and passing before the presumed effigy, could not discover from the guide book what it represented. In the midst of their wonderment Terriss stepped down and caused them much consternation and surprise. The joke is by no means an original one ; but seeing how it has recently found its counterpart in reality, it is worthy of mention.

And now this brief, disjointed, and all unworthy memoir of a "good fellow" and a general favour-ite must be brought to a close ; and it cannot end better than with some beautiful verses which appeared years ago above the name William Terriss.

BREEZY BILL

LONG AGO

Oh ! a wonderful stream is the river of Time,
  As it runs thro' this realm of tears ;
With relentless flow and monotonous rhyme
It surges on with a wave sublime,
  And is merged in the ocean of years.

And winters drift onward like flakes of snow,
  The summers like birds fly between ;
And the years, the short years, they come and they go
On the river's swift tide, with its ebb and its flow,
  As it glides in the shadow and sheen.

There's a magical isle up the river of Time,
  Where the softest airs are playing ;
There's a cloudless sky and a tropical clime,
And a song as sweet as the vesper chime
  In spring when we first went a-maying.

And the name of the island is Long Ago !
  And we find our lost treasures there ;
There are brows of beauty, and bosoms of snow
(Now heaps of dust, though we loved them so) ;
  There are trinkets and tresses of hair :

There are snatches of songs that nobody sings,
  There are words from an infant's prayer ;
There are lutes unswept and harps without strings,
There are broken vows and pieces of rings,
  That our loved ones used to wear :

THE LIFE OF WILLIAM TERRISS

There are hands that waved when we parted last,
  There are eyes never dimmed by tears;
There are heads never bowed to misfortune's blast,
But still stood erect while the storm went past,
  In the long-forgotten years.

But the sunlight is fading for weal or woe,
  And the waters onward pour;
And Time, the destroyer, with one fell blow,
Has sunk our island of " Long Ago "
  In the ocean of " Never More."

Butler & Tanner, The Selwood Printing Works, Frome, and London.

Archibald Constable & Co

publishers to the India Office

2, Whitehall Gardens, Westminster, S.W.

M ESSRS. ARCHIBALD CONSTABLE & CO.'S
CATALOGUE may be obtained post free on
application.

The following is a list of some Authors whose works are published
by ARCHIBALD CONSTABLE & CO. :—

ARBER, Professor Edward, F.S.A.
BAIN, R. NISBET.
BIRRELL, AUGUSTINE, Q.C.,
M.P.
BRYDEN, H. A.
CAMPBELL, Lord ARCHIBALD.
CHAMBERLAIN, Rt. Hon. JO-
SEPH.
COLQUHOUN, ARCHIBALD R.,
F.R.G.S.
CONWAY, SIR WILLIAM MAR-
TIN.
CROOKE, WILLIAM.
CURZON, Rt. Hon. GEORGE N.,
M.P.
DALE, T. F. ("Stoneclink").
de la SIZERANNE, E.
DENT, CLINTON T.
DILKE, The Rt. Hon. CHARLES,
M.P.
DOYLE, A. CONAN.
EARLE, ALICE MORSE.
FORBES-ROBERTSON, FRANCES.
FORD, PAUL LEICESTER.
FREEMAN, R. AUSTIN.
GAIRDNER, JAMES, LL.D.
GALE, NORMAN.
GERARD, DOROTHEA.
GODKIN, G. LAURENCE.
GOFFIC, CHARLES A.
GOMME, G. LAURENCE.
HACKEL, EDUARD.
HANNA, Colonel H. B.

HARRIS, JOEL CHANDLER
("Uncle Remus").
HOLLAND, CLIVE.
LEFARGUE, PHILIP.
LANE-POOLE, STANLEY.
LANKESTER, E. RAY, F.R.S.
LORNE, Marquis of, K.T., M.P.
LOTI, PIERRE.
MACLEOD, FIONA.
MEREDITH, GEORGE.
MEYNELL, ALICE.
MOORE, F. FRANKFORT.
NANSEN, FRIDTJOF, F.R.G.S.
PHILIPS, F. C.
ROBERTS, MORLEY.
SHARP, WILLIAM.
SICHEL, EDITH.
SINCLAIR, Ven. Archdeacon.
STANTON, FRANK L.
STEEL, FLORA ANNIE.
STOKER, BRAM.
STURGIS, JULIAN.
TARVER, JOHN CHARLES.
THOMPSON, FRANCIS.
TREVOR-BATTYE, AUBYN, F.L.S.
VIBART, Colonel HENRY M.
WADDELL, Surgeon-Major, L.A.
WALFORD, L. B.
WARD, A. W., Litt.D.
WARREN, KATE M.
WHITE, GLEESON.
WICKSTEED, PHILIP.
WILKINSON, SPENSER.

ARCHIBALD CONSTABLE & CO

Gaiety Chronicles

By JOHN HOLLINGSHEAD

CONTAINING EARLY PORTRAITS

SIR HENRY IRVING	DAVID JAMES
JOHN L. TOOLE	JOHN CLAYTON
ALFRED WIGAN	FRED LESLIE
EDWARD TERRY	GEORGE EDWARDES
ROBERT SOUTAR	Miss ELLEN FARREN
CHARLES MATTHEWS	Miss KATE VAUGHAN
W. J. FLORENCE	Miss CONSTANCE LOSEBY
SAMUEL EMERY	Mrs. KENDAL
H. E. DIXON	Miss EMILY FOWLER
E. W. ROYCE	Miss E. LITTON
HENRY J. BYRON	Miss ROSE LECLERQ
SAMUEL PHELPS	Miss ADELAIDE NEILSON
DION BOUCICAULT	Miss JULIA MATTHEWS
HERMAN VEZIN	Mrs. JOHN WOOD
CHARLES SANTLEY	Miss CONNIE GILCHRIST
ARTHUR CECIL	(Countess of Orkney)
F. C. BURNAND	SARAH BERNHARDT
SIR ARTHUR SULLIVAN	ETC., ETC

Demy 8vo, 21/-

2, WHITEHALL GARDENS, WESTMINSTER.

ARCHIBALD CONSTABLE & CO

POPULAR 6s. BOOKS.

THE POTENTATE. A Romance. By FRANCES FORBES-ROBERTSON.
Crown 8vo. **6s.**
" There are strong dramatic situations and tragic force in this romance . . . brightly
written."—*The Athenæum.*

ODD STORIES. By FRANCES FORBES-ROBERTSON. Crown 8vo. **6s.**

**THE MACMAHON: OR, THE STORY OF THE SEVEN
JOHNS.** By OWEN BLAYNEY. Crown 8vo. **6s.**
" The book has its action against the historical background of the events which followed
the battle of the Boyne. . . . Told with a rare knowledge of the historical conditions it
describes, and with wit and imagination . . . its subordinate incidents are many and
picturesque . . . strongly conceived and ably written."—*The Scotsman.*

DRACULA. By BRAM STOKER. Crown 8vo. **6s.** Fifth Edition.
" One of the most enthralling and unique romances ever written."—*The Christian World.*
" The idea is so novel that one gasps, as it were, at its originality. A romance far above
the ordinary production."—*St. Paul's.*

ADVENTURES IN LEGEND. Tales of the West Highlands. By the
MARQUIS OF LORNE, K.T., M.P. Fully Illustrated. Crown 8vo. **6s.**
" The Marquis of Lorne has certainly given to the book-reading public much food for quiet
reflection, and a glimpse at the national history of the Highlands, which is a valuable con-
tribution to the literature of the North."—*Whitehall Review.*

**THE VIGIL : A Tale of Adventure in Zululand. By CHARLES MONTAGUE,
Author of "Tales of a Nomad." Fourteen Full-page Illustrations by A. D.
M'CORMICK. 6s.**
" It is not easy to single out the best in a book that is so thoroughly interesting and
absorbing."—*Leeds Mercury.*

THE LAUGHTER OF PETERKIN. Crown 8vo. **6s.** A Re-telling
of Old Stories of the Celtic Wonder-world. A book for young and old. By FIONA
MACLEOD.
" This latest and most excellent piece of work of Miss Macleod's."—*Spectator.*
" To no more skilful hands than those of Fiona Macleod could the re-telling of these old
tales of the Celtic Wonderland have been confided."—*Morning Post.*
" The book is a charming fairy tale."—*Athenæum.*

POPULAR 3s. 6d. BOOKS.

THE FOLLY OF PEN HARRINGTON. By JULIAN STURGIS.
New Edition. **3s. 6d.**
" Bright, piquant, and thoroughly entertaining."—*The World.*
" Will hold its own with any work of the same class that has appeared during the last
half-dozen years."—*The Speaker.*

GREEN FIRE. A Story of the Western Islands. By FIONA MACLEOD,
Author of "The Sin Eater," "Pharais," "The Mountain Lovers," etc., Crown 8vo.
New Edition. **3s. 6d.**
" There are few in whose hands the pure threads have been so skilfully and delicately
woven as they have in Fiona Macleod's."—*Pall Mall Gazette.*

THE DARK WAY OF LOVE. By CHARLES LE GOFFIC. Translated
by WINGATE RINDER. Crown 8vo. **3s. 6d.**
" To state the salient facts of the story can give no idea of the impressiveness of the book.
. . . The work cannot but strongly interest every one who takes it up."—*The Scotsman.*

IN THE TIDEWAY. By FLORA ANNIE STEEL, Author of "On
the Face of the Waters," etc. New Edition. **3s. 6d.**
" This book adds greatly to an established position. It is profoundly impressive."—*St.
James's Budget.*

THE ENEMIES. A Novel. By E. H. COOPER. **3s. 6d.**
" A sober, well-written story, with a strong political flavour, throwing, too, a queer light
on the shady side of Irish elections."—*Daily Graphic.*

HIS VINDICATION. By Mrs. NEWMAN. **3s. 6d.**
" ' His Vindication ' is a capital story."—*Daily Telegraph.*

2, WHITEHALL GARDENS, WESTMINSTER.

NEW BOOKS OF TRAVEL

A Northern Highway of the Tsar

By AUBYN TREVOR-BATTYE,

Author of "Ice-bound on Kolguev." Illustrated. Crown 8vo. **6s.**

"A remarkable achievement . . . the account is graphic to a degree . . . a large public will welcome his book."—*Daily Chronicle.*
". . . This journey, attended by much labour and hardship, and by dangers not a few."—*Scotsman.*

Travel·and Life in Ashanti and Jaman

By R. AUSTIN FREEMAN.

Fully Illustrated from Drawings by the Author and others, and from Photographs. 2 Maps. Demy 8vo. **21s.**

Among the Himalayas

By MAJOR L. A. WADDELL.

With numerous Illustrations by A. D. M'CORMICK, the Author, and others, and from Photographs and Maps. Large Demy 8vo. **21s.**

The Sportswoman's Library

VOLS. I. AND II. EDITED BY FRANCES SLAUGHTER.

Fully Illustrated and containing contributions by Mrs. BURN (*née* ANSTRUTHER-THOMPSON), Mrs. PENN-CURZON, The Hon. Mrs. LANCELOT LOWTHER, The COUNTESS OF MALMESBURY, Mrs. L. W. WYLLIE, Miss WALROND, Miss MAY BALFOUR, the Editor, and others. Sold in single volumes.

"The Game of Polo"

By T. F. DALE ("*Stoneclink*" of "*The Field*").

Illustrated by LILLIAN SMYTHE, CUTHBERT BRADLEY, and CRAWFORD WOOD; and a Photogravure Portrait of Mr. JOHN WATSON.

Demy 8vo. **21s. net.**

"Likely to rank as the standard work on the subject."—*Morning Post.*
"What the author does not know about it is not knowledge."—*Pall Mall Gazette.*
"Will doubtless be of great use to beginners."—*Illustrated Sporting and Dramatic.*
"A charming addition to the library of those who are devoted to the game."—*The Globe.*

8